Death strikes a false note

"Hello?" I said. My voice was thick with sleep. As always happens when the phone rings at an odd hour, I expected the worst possible news.

"Suppose I woke you. Sorry about that."

"It's—it's four-thirty in the morning." I pulled my plaid-flannel sheets and down comforter over my head and pressed my ear against the earpiece. "Who is this?"

"Sheriff Mort Metzger." He sounded offended that I didn't know.

"Why are you calling at this ungodly hour?"

"They found somebody dead up at Worrell."

"Who?" I asked.

"A young woman. 'Bout twenty-nine, thirty. Name's Maureen Beaumont. A classical musician. Played the flute, I think."

"How did she die?"

"Gunshot to the head."

BRANDY & BULLETS

A *Murder, She Wrote* Mystery

A Novel by Jessica Fletcher
& Donald Bain
based on the
Universal television series
created by Peter S. Fisher,
Richard Levinson & William Link

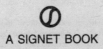

A SIGNET BOOK

SIGNET
Published by the Penguin Group
Penguin Books USA Inc., 375 Hudson Street,
New York, New York 10014, U.S.A.
Penguin Books Ltd, 27 Wrights Lane,
London W8 5TZ, England
Penguin Books Australia Ltd, Ringwood,
Victoria, Australia
Penguin Books Canada Ltd, 10 Alcorn Avenue,
Toronto, Ontario, Canada M4V 3B2
Penguin Books (N.Z.) Ltd, 182–190 Wairau Road,
Auckland 10, New Zealand

Penguin Books Ltd, Registered Offices:
Harmondsworth, Middlesex, England

First published by Signet, an imprint of Dutton Signet,
a division of Penguin Books USA Inc.

First Printing, August, 1995
10 9 8 7 6 5

The first chapter of this book previously appeared in *Rum & Razors*.

Ⓤ REGISTERED TRADEMARK—MARCA REGISTRADA

Printed in the United States of America

PUBLISHER'S NOTE
This is a work of fiction. Names, characters, places, and incidents either are the
product of the author's imagination or are used fictitiously, and any resemblance to
actual persons, living or dead, events, or locales is entirely coincidental.

For my wife, Renée

BRANDY
& BULLETS

Chapter One

"The usual, Jess?"

"Not today, Mara. Spring has sprung and I've sworn off blueberry pancakes. Bikini season's just around the corner."

"*You* wear a bikini?" Mara asked over her shoulder as she drew coffee from a stainless-steel urn behind the counter.

"No. My girlish figure has never been girlish enough to run the risk. But I would like to be able to fit this summer into what bathing suits I do own."

"Aw, come on, honey," said Mara in her usual up-beat voice. "You've got nothing to worry about. You look fabulous. Me? I'm another story. I only eat broken cookies because the broken ones don't have calories. Doesn't work. The hips keep getting bigger, the shoulders smaller. Sure about the pancakes?"

"Yes, I'm sure. But thanks for the compliment. One egg. Over easy. English muffin, dry. Coffee. Skim milk. Sweet'n Low."

"Gorry, Jess," said Seth Hazlitt, Cabot Cove's senior and most popular physician, and my dear friend.

"You sound like the girl in that movie—what was it?—*When Henry Met Sweetie?*"

"*When Harry Met Sally.*"

Cabot Cove's sheriff, Morton Metzger, another good friend, sat up straight and grinned with satisfaction at having come up with the right title. "It's Harry and Sally, Seth. Where'd you get Henry and Sweetie, for cryin' out loud? It's Harry and Sally. Everybody knows that."

There was laughter up and down the counter of Mara's postage stamp-sized luncheonette. Cabot Cove had other larger, and certainly more elegant eating places, but none with the waterfront charm and down-home comfort of Mara's. Somehow, the ripped vinyl chairs and cigar burns on the edge of the counter and tables made the simple, good food taste even better. But probably the most palatable aspect of the small luncheonette was the spirited conversation. Every table, and every stool at the counter held an opinion—on everything. Including movies.

"I loved *When Harry Met Sally,*" Kurt Jones, our local pharmacist with his faded movie-star looks of another era, chimed in. "That was some scene. The two of them were sitting in a restaurant and the girl faked—"

"Yes, that's the same movie, Kurt," I quickly said, hoping to kill the topic. But my attempt breached one of many unwritten rules of debate in Mara's. Nothing was off-limits. If you dared step in for breakfast, you went with the flow.

"That was some funny business," said a lobster fisherman who, until now, had been content to silently attack his overflowing plate of corned-beef hash. His partner, whose weather-beaten face and ink-black fingers defined Maine fisherman, sat next to him. He gave out with a knowing laugh and launched into his critique of the movie's most memorable scene.

I again tried to change the subject. Mara giggled. She'd been serving breakfast to the town's fishermen for almost seventeen years, seven days a week, the doors open at five A.M., the grill fired up by five-thirty. She'd heard it all. And thrived on it.

The men at the counter continued to eat their substantial breakfasts as they launched into a series of risqué comments, punctuated by winks, elbows in the ribs, and explosive laughter. It was obviously more fun talking about Harry and Sally than the hard, cold day they faced out on the Atlantic.

"Finally, a real spring day," I said as Mara served my breakfast. "I saw a robin out my kitchen window this morning."

"Don't get too used to it," said Seth. "Just a tease. You know full well, Jessica, that spring doesn't come to Maine until July."

"July? Try, August," said Kurt, as he put on his coat.

"Another day it'll be colder'n a moose yard," one of the fishermen said.

Kurt bumped into a small table, sending menus to the floor.

"Gawmy SOB, ain't he" came from the fishing contingent at the counter.

Kurt winced at the down east reference to his clumsiness and left.

"I suppose I'm just the eternal optimist," I said. "As far as I'm concerned, spring is here to stay."

"To optimism," said Mort, lifting his glass of fresh-squeezed orange juice.

I returned his toast with my coffee cup.

"Goin' to the press conference tomorrow?" Seth asked.

"Wouldn't miss it," I said.

"Should be interesting to see what this Worrell fella has up his sleeve," said Mort. "Somethin' scandalous most likely. Seems nobody holds a press conference lest there's a scandal to hush up. Last time Cabot Cove had one was what, ten years ago? When the padre announced his resignation after that boy accused him of sexual misconduct."

"We had one more recently than that," said Seth. "Remember? Martha called a conference to announce she was pregnant and was takin' maternity leave from bein' mayor."

"I certainly do," Mort replied, dabbing a moistened corner of his napkin at egg yolk that had slid down his chin and onto his brown uniform tie. "Sorry," he said. "What about you, Jess? Got any inside information on what Worrell's up to?"

"Afraid not. At least nothing official. But I think you rumormongers are going to be disappointed."

"How so?"

"Because from what I hear—and it's strictly hearsay—there's not going to be any scandal involved. My information is that Mr. Worrell is simply going to announce that he's donating Worrell Mansion to Cabot Cove."

"That would be terrific," one of the town's sanitation workers said. He'd been listening to our conversation from a table behind us. "It's some big place. What'll the town do with it?"

I shrugged. "Probably what it's always done with it. Use the grounds for picnics and ball games. The difference will be the town will own it, instead of just having access to it."

"I heard he was going to propose that the town turn it into a nature preserve and museum," another customer offered.

"I didn't hear that," Mara said from where she turned a batch of home fries. "We already have enough nature preserves." She leaned on the counter, and using the greasy spatula for emphasis, said in a conspiratorial voice, "I hear the mansion is going to become a school for the deaf and the blind. Seems that the young Mr. Worrell and his wife have a baby who's hearing impaired."

"What a shame," I said. "Just goes to show money can't buy everything. Here he is with more money than Ross Perot, good-looking, young—couldn't be more than forty—and the only living heir to the Worrell fortune. You'd think he had it all. Then you hear something like this, and you realize that tragedy can hit anyone." I took the napkin from my lap and placed it on the counter. "Breakfast was delicious as usual, Mara."

"Leaving us so soon," Mort asked.

"Yes. Have to run. Literally. A slow jog or fast walk

through Monroe Park. Maybe I'll spot more robins celebrating this lovely day."

"Playing hooky, huh?" Seth said, laughing.

"Yes. I finished the latest book this past weekend and intend to take off some time before starting the next. Taking a breather, as they say. Sound good, Doc?"

"Therapeutic, Jess. That's for certain. Like I always say, if I could write prescriptions for vacations and sabbaticals, I would. Far as this doctor's concerned, stress kills more people than everything else combined."

"Shame health insurance plans don't cover prescriptions for vacations," I said.

"Nothing preventative ever is," Seth added with solemnity.

"That's what's wrong with this new health plan comin' outta Washington," Mort said.

"It's got its good points," said Seth.

"Hell it does," the sanitation man said.

Sensing the beginning of a heated debate, I stood. "Have a wonderful day," I said.

Mort handed me the five-dollar bill I'd left on the counter. "My treat," he said. "Happy spring!"

"Why, thank you, Mort. That's very kind. And yes. Happy spring!"

Chapter Two

"Please, everyone, take your seats so we can get started."

Sybil Stewart, Cabot Cove's new mayor, repeated her request, this time in a louder, more shrill voice. Her frustration at not being able to bring the press conference to order creased her round face into a grimace.

"P-l-e-a-s-e," she implored. "Let's show Mr. Worrell our best Cabot Cove manners."

Sybil, who had always been an unabashed Nancy Reagan fan, including Ms. Reagan's taste in fashion, smoothed the pleats on the skirt of her tailored crimson suit as she waited for order. Her suit and blouse were strictly big-city. Her red pumps were small-town.

A few people stopped their animated conversations and took their seats, but most ignored Sybil's pleas. I looked around the congested room and couldn't help but smile. Interest in today's announcement seemed to have drawn all of Cabot Cove, as well as people whose faces were unfamiliar to me. No surprise, actually. Like most New Englanders, our town's citizens *love* to talk about politics. Whether I'm waiting in line at Store 24 or having dinner at any of Cabot Cove's restaurants, eavesdropping on conversations around me invariably picks up snippets of political debate. And not just local political talk. National politics, too. In the blood, I suppose. Or the clam chowder.

Jared Worrell, the reason for the press conference, stood quietly behind Sybil. Although this was the first time he'd been to Cabot Cove, he dressed like he belonged. His sport jacket was preppy muted-brown tweed. He wore tan slacks with a crease that would cut cheese, pale blue button-down shirt, subtly striped green-and-brown tie, and penny-loafers. His Roman nose and square jawline hinted at aristocracy, like a Kennedy. Although he lived in Southern California—Beverly Hills I'd heard—he was not my vision of a "Muscle Beach" surfer. He was quite short, thin, and pale. I judged him to be in his early thirties.

Since the death of the Worrell family's patriarch more than a hundred years ago, the mansion had been held in a trust agreement with Cabot Cove that stipulated that as long as the town maintained it, its use as a conference center, park, and playground was to be enjoyed by all the town's citizens. And enjoy it we did, along with the tourists who traveled to our sleepy village on the ocean to soak up the grandeur of another time. L.L. Bean in Freeport and lobster dinners up and down Maine's coast would always be bigger attractions. But Worrell had its share of out-of-town admirers, and the local economy benefited from their tourist dollars. Whether what Mr. Worrell would announce this morning would change things was why we'd all shown up at city hall—to hear first-hand what the future held.

As the last surviving family member, Jared Worrell had come to town to fulfill the terms of the trust agreement. Every five years, on the sixteenth of March, the senior surviving member of the Worrell family was free to discontinue the trust agreement, and to sell the property. Until this day, the senior surviving member had been Jared's elder sister, Waldine, who would always send a letter informing us that the agreement would remain in force for another five years. But Waldine Worrell had died the previous summer. It was now Jared's responsibility to make the decision about his ancestors' family mansion. That he'd decided to come in person made townspeople nervous. If he was going to extend the trust agreement, all he had to do was write a letter as his sister had done. Then again, some reasoned, he might have decided to personally appear in order to bask in the limelight of announcing that the mansion would be donated outright to Cabot Cove. Glass half-full, or half-empty? The speculation would cease in a few minutes, when Jared Worrell officially put an end to it.

"Quiet everyone!" Sybil Stewart had given up trying to cajole the crowd to attention. She fairly yelled into the microphone, and her new approach worked. She was a woman to be reckoned with. The room became relatively silent.

"Thank you. As you all know, Jared Worrell has

come to Cabot Cove to make an announcement about the future of the Worrell Mansion. If you're wondering whether I've been made privy to what he is about to say, I assure you I haven't been. Among many of Mr. Worrell's admirable traits, discretion is obviously one of them." She glanced at Worrell, who smiled. Not a big smile. Just a hint. He stood straight, hands at his sides, his eyes slowly scanning the room. A self-assured man, I thought. Great wealth always helps establish such confidence.

Sybil continued, "I know that Mr. Worrell has a busy schedule and must leave immediately following his remarks. So I won't take any more time. Mr. Worrell."

Worrell stepped to the podium, glanced down at an index card, said, "Thank you for all being here. I know how important my family's residence has been to Cabot Cove. I also know that there is understandable concern in this room about the future of Worrell Mansion. Let me assure you that you will be happy to hear what I have to say this morning."

Sybil tried to initiate a round of applause, but her hands were the only ones to be heard. The faces around me were serious. You don't tell someone from Maine that he'll be happy, and expect him to applaud. Like people from Missouri, and I suppose just about everywhere else, telling us to be happy doesn't work. "Show me!"

Jared sipped water from a glass and continued: "Too often, stately houses and sprawling grounds end up in the hands of greedy developers who only see such properties as sites for intrusive condominiums and ugly shopping malls. That will not be the case with my family's home and gardens."

This time, Sybil's applause was joined by a scattering of others.

"I am pleased to announce today that the Worrell Mansion has been sold to the Corcoran Group, an investment banking group based in Boston."

There were groans, and a few boos.

Worrell held up his hands and gave another small smile. "I know what you're thinking," he said. "But hear me out. The Corcoran Group is a prestigious and community-conscious organization. Its development record in Boston is pristine, and worthy of civic pride. I did not sell the mansion to the Corcoran Group without attaching strings. There will be no condos, no shopping malls. The sale assures that my family's residence will become a retreat for writers, artists, and musicians."

I sat in the rear of the room because I'd arrived a few minutes late. My friends, Seth and Mort, were up front. The expressions on most faces were disbelief and dismay. The gap between Jared Worrell and his audience was wide. As far as he was concerned, keeping Worrell Mansion from becoming a mall or housing development was worthy of a standing ovation. From the perspective of the Cabot Cove citizens who crowded the room, anything short of the status quo was a blow. The mansion was being sold. A retreat for artists and writers? What did *that* mean?

"For those of you who are skeptical of what I've just announced, let me elaborate, and put you at ease. The Worrell Institute for Creativity, which will be its official name, will become a sanctuary where writers and artists can come for inspiration, in much the same way this great estate's solace and beauty has inspired many of you through the years. It will attract great writers and artists, as well as fledgling writers and artists who might one day be great.

"Many of its rooms will be converted into guest rooms and suites. The conference center will be used in much the same capacity it has for decades, a setting for seminars, workshops, and other creative endeavors. There will also be, I understand, numerous functions each year to which you, the public, will be invited, indeed urged to attend. While the institute will be privately owned, it is the desire of the Corcoran people that it be an interactive facility with the good citizens of this community."

"How do we interact with a bunch 'a weirdo writers?" one of our crusty citizens tossed at Worrell.

Worrell laughed gently. "I promise you'll have the opportunity to ask questions when I've completed my statement."

He continued: "The eighty acres of land that surround the mansion will be preserved just as it is. That is to say, there won't be any development of it. The land and gardens will be used by those in residence for walks and inspiration. I can envision writers choosing to bring their laptop computers into the gardens, perhaps to sit under a tree and create great novels and poems." He laughed, alone. "I have no idea how writers work, but I do know that they need inspiration. I believe that this magnificent place that was once the home of my family, and that has played such an important part in your lives, will be revived into a vital cultural center, a place of inspiration for the men and women who create our works of art, and for each of you as you claim, with pride, that Cabot Cove has become a revered and international cultural city. That concludes my prepared statement. I have time for a few questions." He glanced at two men and a woman who stood at the side of the room. The woman pointed to her watch. Worrell nodded.

"What about the playground?"

"Yes. What about the children of Cabot Cove?" shouted a thirtyish woman in the front row, whose loud, offensive voice was well-known to all of us. Her question was met with applause, and a chorus of "Hear! Hear!"

Jared took another sip of water and smacked his lips. "Let me just say that all the specifics haven't been worked out yet. However, as a parent, I know the importance of parks and playgrounds, and I have made that known to the Corcoran Group. I'm confident that even though existing playgrounds might have to be moved, room will be found on the property for a new playground, larger and better equipped than the current one."

An elderly gentleman stood. Walter was a retired physics teacher at our local community college. His voice was deep and resonant. "Mr. Worrell," he intoned, "it is my understanding that at these type of writers' retreats, a lot more sex goes on than writing."

A few uncertain snickers circled the room.

Jared replied, "I wouldn't know about that, sir. But I assure you that the new owners will see to it that the Worrell Institute for Creativity is a place for writers to write, and for artists to create. Next."

One of our mailmen, Jerry Monk, who'd been delivering to my house for a few years, stood. He was overweight, and totally bald, and he spoke with the labored breathing that overweight invariably causes. "Mr. Worrell, no offense. But we all know that writers drink a lot, and even use drugs. That's common knowledge. No secret about it. They have to, I hear, to keep writing their stories." He looked at the people next to him before adding, "Sounds to me like this town is going to pot."

Laughter, and applause.

I had to say something. I'm a writer. I enjoy an occasional glass of wine with dinner. I've never used drugs in my life.

I stood. "Sir, if I might," I said, hopefully loud enough to cut through the noise. People turned and looked at me. "My name is Jessica Fletcher. As a writer of more than thirty novels, I feel compelled to take issue with the mistaken perception expressed here this morning about writers and artists. I assure any of you who share Jerry Monk's view of us—of me—that you're wrong. Believe me, your concerns and fears about having creative people in residence at this new institute are unfounded."

I expected some response. There wasn't any. Just stares. I took a deep breath and continued: "Ladies and gentlemen, I personally know just about all of you. We've shared many years together in this town that we love. Frankly—and I understand your concerns—I believe that what Mr. Worrell has presented us today, that his family's ancestral home will become the Worrell Institute for Creativity, could prove to be a positive thing for Cabot Cove. It could spawn a cultural center of which we can all be proud. I—endorse it, and I hope you will, too."

I sat and thought about what I'd just said. I hadn't intended to endorse this new use of the Worrell Mansion. All I wanted to do was defend writers. The endorsement just came out.

A few people applauded my comments, led by Seth and Morton.

Jared Worrell smiled appreciatively. "Thank you, Mrs. Fletcher. I'm well aware of your reputation as an author, and I'm honored that you're here. I didn't know you were a bona fide Cabot Cove resident. Maybe we should consider renaming the institute the Fletcher Institute for Creativity."

Jared's comment elicited loud applause, again initiated by Seth and Mort. I'm sure I turned the color of Sybil's suit and shoes. It's not my style to draw attention to myself.

Sybil Stewart officially ended the conference. As I made my way to Seth and Mort, I became aware that my remarks hadn't been unanimously well received. Some people extended their hands and told me they agreed with what I'd said, but most fixed me with icy stares.

Seth, Morton, and I left city hall together. We

stood on the sidewalk and watched Jared Worrell and his entourage climb into a black stretch limousine with blackened windows that had been idling in the circular drive. The window suddenly opened, and Jared poked his head out. "Got to catch a plane, Mrs. Fletcher. On my way to Bangor Airport. Thanks for your support."

I waved.

I'd invited Mort and Seth to join me, and a friend from Boston, Julie, for chowder at my house. We were on our way to where Seth's car was parked when Sybil Stewart's voice stopped us. We waited for her to catch up.

"Thanks for waiting, Jess. I didn't know it before, but it's obvious you're all for this so-called institute. I just want to tell you that you're very much in the minority. Most people are angry, and I feel it's my obligation to support them. I've called an emergency town council meeting here at city hall tomorrow morning at nine. We need to discuss how we're going to deal with what Mr. Worrell has announced. I had no idea he intended to turn his family's home, for God's sake, into a den of iniquity. I now know that you and I are on opposite sides of this fence. But I'm not alone, as you could see. There's a lot of opposition to it because it could be the demise of Cabot Cove. I feel strongly it needs to be addressed by the entire council."

Will she come up for air? I wondered.

"Do me a personal favor, Jess, and attend tomorrow's meeting. Maybe we can convince our leading creative citizen that this institute will be the worst possible thing for Cabot Cove."

"I'm always willing to listen, Sybil. You know that. I'll be there."

Chapter Three

A Few Weeks Later

If I've ever questioned why I'm not politically involved, the "emergency meeting" of the town council two weeks ago concerning the Worrell Institute for Creativity answered it for me.

I showed up early and joined dozens of other citizens. The ten-person council, four men and six women, flanked Sybil as she sat at the center of three long, folding tables. An assortment of plastic coffee cups from Mara's Luncheonette left rings on the tabletops, and on blank yellow legal pads.

Sybil was a woman possessed. As commander-in-chief of our town, this was to be her political milestone, the defense of Cabot Cove. Rally the troops. Circle the wagons. We were on the eve of war. The writers and artists were poised on the other side of the hill for a frontal assault. Don't shoot until you see the white of their pages, the colors on their palettes.

For me, the most immediate danger was a threatened strike by our garbage collectors. Don't be cynical, Jessica. Hear them out.

Which I did, wincing as Sybil read a speech she'd

obviously labored long and hard over the previous night: ". . . And so, my friends and fellow citizens, I implore each of you to join your elected officials in mounting an effective counterattack against this assault on our treasured way of life, a threat to our children, and a perversion of our values."

"Is it really that bad?" asked a member of the council, a farmer whose annual hayrides were the highlight of every Cabot Cove Halloween. "Hell, Sybil, what I mean is, I got a nephew down in New York who's a writer. Pretty good one, too, I hear. Nice young chap. Doesn't drink or smoke. Real polite young man."

Sybil could barely contain her annoyance. She sighed, slowly shook her head, and said, "There are always exceptions, Rufus. Individually, I suppose creative people can be all right." I coughed. She looked at me, raised her eyebrows into arches, and continued: "The problem arises, Rufus, when creative people gather together. That's when pornography, orgies, drunken rumbles, and the like occur, when they have nothing to do but indulge in those things."

Rufus was not to be dismissed. "That's all they do, Sybil, have parties? When does anything get written?"

"After they go home," she said. And then, as though a sudden brilliant thought had struck her, she added, "Yes, there might be some writing that goes on. Even erotic poetry is considered writing."

I was desperate to leave. I couldn't believe what I was hearing. I was aware, of course, that Cabot Cove was a conservative community, steeped in what probably would be considered old-fashioned values. In most instances, I shared those values, and was glad I lived in a town where they existed.

But there is a difference between old-fashioned values, and straight-out prejudice and broad-brush smearing of classes of people—any class of people. I was in the process of rationalizing to myself that Sybil's behavior was an aberration, that reason would ultimately prevail, when she said, "Jessica Fletcher, as we all know, is a respected mystery writer. Not the sort who goes to writers' camps. Yesterday, we heard Mrs. Fletcher speak out at the press conference on Mr. Worrell's behalf. Now that she's had time to sleep on it, I'm certain she realizes that our concerns about the Worrell Institute are justified."

Being put on the spot like that offended me, as did the assumption that I'd come to my senses. I stood. "I'm afraid you're wrong, Sybil. I haven't changed my view any more than you have. Excuse me. I must go."

No one said anything as I put on my raincoat and headed for the door at the rear of the room. But I stopped, turned, and said, "What bothers me is that assumptions are being made before the institute opens and its residents arrive. Are we that closed-minded that we aren't willing to give it a chance?"

Men on the council fiddled with their empty cups, and removed imaginary lint from winter-worn sweaters and jackets. A few coughed nervously. A council member, Sue Maehart, a good friend, smiled and nodded.

Buoyed by her encouragement, I went on: "I did

not intend to say anything this morning. But as long as I've made an effort to be here, I do have something to say. All writers are not drunks. Nor are they sexaholics. Some writers drink. Some even enjoy sex, I hear." Several in the room laughed. Sybil was not amused.

"And, yes, some writers drink *and* enjoy sex. But, I also hear that there are lawyers, doctors, plumbers, teachers, scientists, and astronauts who do, too."

"She's right about that," a man muttered to his wife. "Especially the lawyers."

"I love this town and its people," I said. "But would anyone deny that we could use a cultural boost? We have our movie theater. And the high school drama productions are always darn good. But the Worrell Institute for Creativity could establish Cabot Cove as a cultural center to be envied. It will draw talented men and women to our community, writers and artists, poets and essayists. Eventually, it might become the cultural mecca of New England. But only if we stand behind it. Or, at least, not kill its potential before it has a chance to get off the ground.

"You talk of our children. Many of Cabot Cove's children could be gifted writers, only they don't know it because it hasn't been nurtured in them. A place like the Worrell Institute can inspire them." I paused. "It can inspire the writer in all of us."

Sue Maehart applauded. Others joined.

"Finally," I said, "if I haven't changed your minds, consider this. No matter what you think or say, the mansion has been sold to this Corcoran Group in

Boston. It will become a creative center. That is the reality. And I suggest we get on to more pressing matters—like who will collect our garbage next week."

I opened the door.

"Jessica?"

I turned. "Yes, Sybil?"

"I didn't know that great writers were supposed to be great speakers as well."

I sighed, smiled. "Just another misconception, Sybil. But thank you for the compliment."

I left realizing that I had finally become involved in politics.

Stick to writing was the advice I gave myself.

And so spring turned to summer in Cabot Cove, and I started work on my new novel. Everything gets used by a writer, they say. Every life experience, every person met. I'm no exception. I started each day that spring and summer by taking a long walk up to the Worrell Mansion, where construction crews busily renovated the stately old queen into what it would become—the Worrell Institute for Creativity. Huge earth-moving machines and dozens of men (and a few women who wore their hard hats with equal pride as their male counterparts) transformed the mansion. The tranquil summer was punctuated by the whine of power saws, and the hammering of nails. Representatives of the Corcoran Group conferred with architects. Progress was afoot in sleepy Cabot Cove, and it was met with mixed reactions.

Overall, the clamor against the institute had pretty

much abated. Many townspeople found work with the construction gangs. Mara saw an opportunity. She rented a small truck, outfitted it with a coffee urn, loaded it with Danish and sandwiches, and brought her luncheonette to the site to feed the hungry crews. Every motel within ten miles was booked to capacity. While there were still those who grumbled about what was to become of Cabot Cove once the institute opened in the fall, most chose not to look this gift horse in its mouth.

And I found inspiration in the Worrell Mansion that summer. My new novel would revolve around a murder that takes place in a creative artists' retreat that has been established in a small New England town. I told no one of this, of course, lest they think I intended to profit from this new chapter in Cabot Cove's life story.

Which, of course, was exactly what I was doing.

I toyed with various titles as I progressed on the book. *Artists in Crime. The Creative Murders. Creativity Most Foul.* None of which pleased me. Eventually, the book would be called *Brandy & Bullets.* But that part of the story is still to come.

Chapter Four

Autumn—That Same Year

Autumn, my favorite time of year, always arrives earlier in Maine than other parts of New England. This year, it came earlier than ever. The clear blue sky seemed bigger and higher; the air had a crispness that was welcome after an unusually warm and humid summer. Soon, winter would roar into Maine with its customary fury. But for now, perfection reigned.

One of my favorite rites of passage each fall has been to take a five-mile walk through Cabot Creek Preserve, a wildlife refuge with soaring, full trees that boast the most vibrant primary colors during peak foliage. That's what I did this morning. I took along my binoculars with hopes of spotting any of the myriad species of birds that top the endangered species list, a few of which have historically called the preserve home. I had no such luck. I could only hope they hadn't yet joined the extinction list.

The picture-perfect weekend weather forecast received rave reviews from local inns, and bed-and-breakfasts; NO VACANCY signs were up everywhere as tourists drove hundreds of miles to marvel at what

I've always been able to enjoy from my kitchen window.

But tourists and townspeople weren't the only ones to thank Mother Nature for a splendid weekend. The official opening of the Worrell Institute for Creativity was scheduled for that night. Renovations on the mansion had been completed only days ago, and last-minute touch-ups were still going on. Resistance to the center had continued to decline, although there were still a few vocal citizens who spoke against it at every opportunity. Mara's Luncheonette was their favorite forum, which was why I'd been eating most of my breakfasts at home. Sybil Stewart had eased off on her public condemnation of the mansion's new use, which gave her time to settle the threatened garbage strike, and to focus on other more pressing town matters. Evidently, my little speech had had some impact upon her thinking, especially the part in which I pointed out that no matter what anyone thought, or felt, the center was about to become a reality. "It's a no-win situation," she was widely quoted as saying whenever the subject came up. Which, of course, it was. We continued to be friendly, although I did discern a certain coolness on her part. Maybe the gala black-tie party to be held that night at the mansion, to which we both were invited, would serve to lessen any tensions. Nothing like champagne and caviar to heal wounds.

I'd just returned from my walk and, over a cup of tea, was debating whether to rake what leaves had already fallen, when the phone rang. "Hello, Seth," I said. "Change your mind?"

"Ayuh. Wouldn't have, except I don't want to see you without an escort tonight."

It seemed that virtually every citizen of Cabot Cove had been invited to the party, at least those with high visibility. But Seth hadn't received an invitation, and I'd asked him to be my "date." My invitation had been addressed to **Mrs. Jessica Fletcher and Guest.**

At first, Seth had declined my offer. "Who wants to go to all the bother of renting a tuxedo?" he'd said. "Doesn't make any sense anyway that it's a black-tie party. You think those writers and artists who've already shown up will be wearin' tuxedos? More like blue jeans and T-shirts."

I agreed with him, although it didn't seem to me to be an especially important issue. What others wore was irrelevant.

But then he said something that gave me better insight into his reluctance. "Should be pretty funny seein' Mort in a tuxedo." His chuckle was forced. "Never seen him out of his uniform." Another laugh. "Probably just stand in a corner like a statue."

Our sheriff, Morton Metzger, had been invited to the party, and accepted. I certainly understood why the institute's directors would want our sheriff on their side. But Seth was Cabot Cove's leading physician. Not inviting him was a slight, in my opinion, or, at best, an oversight. The result? Seth was hurt.

"That's wonderful news," I said. "Have you rented a tux?"

"Ayuh. Harry had one fits me like a glove. Didn't have to change a thing."

"Great. I'm so glad you changed your mind."

"Like I said, Jessica, I didn't want to see you without a proper escort. Mort wouldn't be much of one."

I contained a laugh, simply said, "I'm really looking forward to being on your arm this evening, Doctor. And wear comfortable shoes. I understand there'll be dancing."

The circular drive leading up to the imposing Worrell Mansion was lined with illuminair lights—candles in paper bags with cutout designs. The effect was elegant. A near-full moon, a heavenly floodlight, washed the large stone mansion with white light. A dozen valet parking attendants scurried from car to car. The line was long. We waited our turn behind the stream of cars inching toward the entrance.

"I feel like I'm in Hollywood, not Cabot Cove," said Seth as he put his Toyota Corolla in park. "It'll be a half hour 'fore we get to the door. Never seen so many cars in one place in Cabot Cove before. Looks like the whole damn town was invited, 'cept—"

I smiled and touched his arm. He was still stinging from not having been invited. "Probably a lot of out-of-towners," I said. "From Boston. Maybe New York. From what I hear, the invitation list in Cabot Cove was very small."

"It was?" he said, shifting into gear and covering another few feet of driveway.

"Yes. It was." I hoped that made him feel better.

We finally reached a parking attendant, a young man who I recognized from town. " 'Evening, Mrs. Fletcher," he said as he opened the door for me and helped me maneuver my floor-length black skirt out of the car. "Hello," I said. "Dr. Hazlitt," he said. "Hello, Billy," said Seth. "Sticks in gear at times. Don't strip 'em."

"No, sir."

"Name, sir?" Seth was asked the question by an Olympic-sized young man positioned just outside the front door.

"Hazlitt. Dr. Seth Hazlitt."

Mr. Universe glanced quickly through a sheaf of papers. "Name, again, sir? You're not on the guest list."

"Fletcher. Jessica," I said. "We're together."

Without looking again at the list of names, he said, "This way, ma'am. Sorry for the delay, sir." I smiled at Seth, who looked unimpressed.

"The President here tonight?" Seth muttered as we passed into a wide, long foyer with a ceiling far above our heads. "Why all the tight security?"

"Undoubtedly to protect you from assassins."

Once inside, we were passed along a lengthy receiving line. At its end were the Worrell Institute for Creativity's director, Dr. Michael O'Neill, and his administrative assistant, Beth Anne Portledge.

"Mrs. Fletcher. We are extremely honored to have your presence here this evening," O'Neill said.

"We've been anxiously awaiting your arrival." O'Neill was sixty-something, with a healthy head of silver hair, ruddy cheeks, and seductive, watery blue eyes. No debate about his family's national origins. Irish through and through.

"Welcome to Worrell," Ms. Portledge said pleasantly. She was short and borderline chubby, with a round face, minimal makeup, and straight brown hair pulled back into a tight chignon. She was dressed more for a business meeting than a party. Brown suit with narrow white stripes, white blouse with a large bow at the neck, and sensible brown shoes.

"Thank you very much, Dr. O'Neill," I said. "This is my friend, Dr. Seth Hazlitt."

"Always nice to meet a fellow practitioner," said O'Neill. "Specialty?"

"Family medicine."

"Not enough of you to go around. I practiced family medicine once. Before going into psychiatry."

I hoped Seth wouldn't launch into one of his condemnations of psychiatry. He didn't, to my relief.

Although guests continued to come through the door, O'Neill and his assistant abandoned their spot on the receiving line and took us aside. "I'm looking forward to some good conversations with you, Mrs. Fletcher," O'Neill said. "You're obviously an extremely creative person. All writing is creative, but developing a murder mystery must rank high on the creativity list."

"Actually, I think it's more a case of perspiration than inspiration," I said.

"Modest. But I think there's more to it than that. I've been studying the creative process for many years. I've traveled the world trying to identify just what makes the creative mind work. That's what brings me to Worrell. We're going to focus sharply on the creative processes used by the artists-in-residence."

"Fascinating," I said. I could have added "surprising." It sounded more like group therapy than an artist's retreat.

"Nice meeting you, Doctor," Seth said, taking my elbow. He was obviously anxious to move on.

"The ballroom is just over here," said O'Neill. "Beth Anne, would you be kind enough to hold the fort while I escort this lovely lady to the party?"

The ballroom was already crowded with elegantly dressed people, few of whom I recognized. I spotted Cabot Cove mayor Sybil Stewart, who wore a fancy red gown and who chatted with a knot of guests. An orchestra that sounded like all society ball orchestras played bouncy show tunes, which had a number of couples spinning about the dance floor. It was all very festive, hardly what I expected at a party to open a creative center. I expected any moment to see a line of debs come down the winding staircase.

"Save me a dance," Dr. O'Neill said.

"My pleasure," I said.

He returned to the foyer. A waitress passed with a tray of caviar canapés and stuffed mushrooms. Seth stopped her and loaded up a cocktail napkin with her wares. I nibbled on a canapé as he lightened a waiter's tray by taking two glasses of champagne from it. I raised my glass. "To fall," I said.

"To winter," he said, frowning. "Dance?" The orchestra was playing a favorite of mine, "Just in Time."

"Rain check," I said, continuing to observe the crowd. "There's Mort."

"Where?" Seth stood on tiptoes.

"On the dance floor. With the blond lady."

Seth followed the direction of my finger and saw our friend, Cabot Cove's sheriff, dancing with a woman who was a few inches taller, many years younger, and who looked as though she'd stood in a mold while her silver-and-black-sequined dress was poured over her.

"Be damned," Seth mumbled.

"He looks nice in his tux," I said.

"Looks like a—I suppose he looks okay."

"And having a wonderful time."

"Uh-huh."

Friends from Cabot Cove approached, and we happily chatted: "Beautiful renovation"—"Lovely party"—"So exciting having artists in our town"—"Best party since New Year's Eve of nineteen-eighty"—"Who's the blonde with Sheriff Metzger?"

Before that final question could be answered, Nelson Whippet, Cabot Cove's wealthiest citizen (junk bonds on Wall Street) spirited me to the dance floor, leaving Seth looking lonely and forlorn, even though he was surrounded by friends.

After a series of spirited dips and swirls, Nelson

brought me back to where Seth was now talking with Mort Metzger, and others.

"Whew!" I said, wiping my damp face. "Nelson takes dancing as seriously as his investments."

"You look real nice, Jess," Mort said.

"Thank you."

The slinky blonde was at his side.

Mort realized we were all looking at her. He said, "This here is Susan Dalton. She's a writer. Stayin' here at the institute. Writing a murder mystery."

Susan smiled. "I admit it," she said. "I am picking the brain of a real live law enforcement officer. A real live sheriff."

Morton beamed.

My reaction was one of disbelief. Other artists-in-residence at the party were readily discernible from the other guests. No tuxedos. No patent shoes. No sequined gowns. Their uniforms were jeans, turtlenecks, and corduroy jackets with patches at the elbows.

"Do you have a publisher?" I asked. I wasn't prying. I was interested.

"My brother has a friend who said he would look at the book once I write it. I've been trying to write it for ten years." A giggle. "I hope being here will help."

"I'm sure it will," I said.

"Jessica is a mystery writer," Morton said.

Her eyes opened wide. "You are? Have I read any of your books?"

"I—probably not."

As Seth and I walked away, I heard her say to

Mort, "Jessica Fletcher? I've never heard of her." Which was just as well.

We continued to enjoy the party. The food was excellent (a fancy Boston caterer), and there was an unending supply of it: oysters on the half shell, oysters Rockefeller, pâté, deviled eggs, marinated artichoke hearts, shrimp wontons, crabmeat stuffed mushrooms, calamari, and more. Morton's blond friend had deserted him for a tall, slender man who was identified as one of the institute's psychiatrists. His name sounded Hungarian to me—Tomar Meti— although it could have been of any slavic origin. He *looked* Hungarian; black hair plastered to his head, closely cropped salt-and-pepper beard, probing dark eyes. And a good dancer. Ms. Dalton seemed to be enjoying herself.

"Mrs. Fletcher."

I turned to face Beth Anne, the institute's assistant director.

"Dr. O'Neill thought you might enjoy a personal tour of the facilities."

"That would be lovely."

"The other guests will be shown around," she said. "But Dr. O'Neill asked me to escort you and a few other selected guests on a more comprehensive tour."

I looked at Seth.

"Dr. Hazlitt is welcome, too," Beth Anne said.

"Thank you," Seth said. "You go ahead, Jess. Mort and I still have some eating to do." It was good to see them acting like good friends again. They went off in pursuit of a waiter carrying a large tray of shrimp, and I followed Beth Anne to where a half dozen others waited. Among them was Sybil Stewart, and the county's district attorney, Arthur Goldberg.

We began at the back of the mansion where an expansive greenhouse housed a European spa, replete with an anti-cellulite massage room. Another glass wing connected to the spa contained a heated Olympic-size swimming pool. "Nothing like a couple of laps to cure writer's block," Beth Anne said pleasantly.

"I'm really impressed," I said. "But how much does it cost an artist or writer to stay at Worrell? With all these extravagant amenities, I imagine it isn't cheap."

"We work on a sliding scale," she replied. "Dr. O'Neill would be a better source of that information for you. He'll quote you the rates."

Rates? It was sounding and looking more like a resort every minute.

We passed through the spa again, which smelled like eucalyptus, and entered a long, narrow, winding hallway. "We'll take a quick peek at one of the guest rooms," Portledge said. "I know that Nineteen is empty. There are sixty in all. We have almost a full house."

As we made our way toward Room 19, two things struck me as odd. First, there was a set of French doors with a fancy engraved brass plaque that read: "BEHAVIORAL SCIENCES UNIT." I asked Beth Anne about it.

"We do a lot of work with behavior modification," she answered quickly over her shoulder.

"What kind?" I asked, keeping step.

"The usual. Helping our clients get over whatever

creative problems they might be having. We have special accommodations for those who are really struggling."

She knew her script well.

The second thing that piqued my interest was at the end of the hall, where a small, handwritten sign read: "ADDICTIONS CENTER." Beth Anne's face turned into a scowl as she pulled the sign down and shoved it in her jacket pocket.

I stopped in front of the door as the others continued to follow her. Sensing that she'd lost one person, she stopped and glared at me.

"Mrs. Fletcher?"

"Addictions?" I said. "Alcoholism? That sort of thing?"

"In case we were to have such a problem. We don't!"

In contrast to the opulent public rooms, Room 19 was Zen-like. The walls were stark white; one black-and-white print of a snowy landscape was the only thing to break the white expanse. A white bedspread with tiny pink flowers neatly covered a single bed. A tiny, two-drawer white dresser was on one wall, an equally small, white Formica desk on the other.

"Spartan," DA Goldberg said.

"Functional," Portledge said, leading us from the room. "As few distractions as possible. We want them to spend as little time in their rooms as possible."

I was about to comment that as a writer, the more time spent alone in my room, the more I'd get written. But I didn't express that thought. I'd developed a feeling that Ms. Portledge preferred show-and-tell, without questions from her class.

We reached one of two libraries, whose rich, oak paneling, floor-to-ceiling stacks of books, oversize armchairs, and large wooden desks made them considerably more inviting than Room 19 had been.

Immediately off the library was a sundry-type store that sold magazines and books, supplies, drugstore items, and other necessities found in shopping concourses of the world's grand hotels. There was even a laundry and dry-cleaning service. If Cabot Cove's merchants expected a lot of business from the institute's residents, they were in for a disappointment.

Especially restaurant owners.

The main dining room, or Thoreau Room, as it was called, served three meals daily. The smaller dining room, the Proust Room, served lighter fare all day long, including early-morning continental breakfast and late-night snacks.

"Twenty-four-hour room service," someone in the group said in disbelief when Beth Anne mentioned it.

"Yes. Creative people don't follow the same clock as most others. We try to accommodate."

Dr. O'Neill was waiting when Beth Anne delivered us back to the ballroom. "Enjoy your tour?" he asked me.

"Very much. The services you offer are remarkable."

"Just following some old, wise advice, Mrs. Fletcher. Anything worth doing is worth doing right. Might I speak with you for a moment?"

"Of course."

We went to a relatively quiet corner of the large room. "Mrs. Fletcher—"

"Please. Make it Jessica."

His eyes sparkled. "And my name is Michael. Would you consider teaching a few seminars, maybe two a year, for our residents? You don't need to answer now. But will you at least think about it? We're honored that you live in Cabot Cove."

"That's a fascinating offer," I said.

"We'll compensate you handsomely."

"I will. Think about it, that is."

"Splendid. That's all I ask. Why not give me a call in a few days. We can discuss it further."

"I will."

"Ready for dinner?"

"Dinner?" I laughed. "There's more food to come? I'm already overfed."

"Always room for a little more good food, Jessica."

Seth and Mort had already navigated the long tables overflowing with racks of lamb, prime rib, lobster, and dozens of other beautifully prepared and presented dishes. Using my five-mile walk of that morning as rationalization, I sampled a few items, then danced, more for the exercise than the lure of the music. Finally, Seth and I decided it was time to head home. We said our goodbyes, waited outside for the parking attendant to bring Seth's car from where it had been parked, and we drove down the driveway toward the main gate where we were stopped by a uniformed guard who scrutinized us, wrote down the license plate number, and waved us through.

"Like visitin' the CIA," Seth muttered.

"Yes," I said. "I was thinking the same thing. Enjoy yourself? Glad you came?"

"Sort of."

"It's an impressive operation, isn't it?"

He grunted. "Something not quite right about it," he said. "Not quite real."

I laughed. "Certainly not real, as in Cabot Cove. Can't wait to get home and take off these shoes."

"And me, this damn tuxedo."

"Nightcap?" I asked as we pulled up in front of my house.

"No, ma'am, but thank you. Look at that, Jessica."

I looked at what he pointed to, the lights of the Worrell Mansion glimmering faintly from its hilltop perch on the outskirts of town.

"Pretty," I said.

"Ayuh. And strange. But what can you expect from a bunch of crazy shrinks? Thanks for bringin' me, Jessica. Always proud to be on your arm."

Chapter Five

"Hello?" I said. My voice was thick with sleep. As always happens when the phone rings at an odd hour, I expected the worst possible news.

"Suppose I woke you. Sorry about that."

"It's—it's four-thirty in the morning." The lamp on my night table was still on. The book that had kept me up until a few hours ago, and that had been resting on my chest when my eyes finally closed, had fallen off when I reached for the phone. I pulled my plaid flannel sheets and down comforter over my head, and pressed my ear against the earpiece.

"Who is this?"

"Mort." He sounded offended that I didn't know. "Sorry it's so early."

"You already said that. It's all right. But why are you calling at this ungodly hour?"

"They found somebody dead up at Worrell."

"What? Is this a bad dream?"

"It's no bad dream you're having, Jessica." He laughed. "I said somebody's been found dead at the Worrell Institute." He sounded eerily jubilant considering the time of day, and the circumstances.

"Who?" I asked.

"A young woman. 'Bout twenty-nine, thirty. Name's Maureen Beaumont. A classical musician. Played the flute, I think."

"How did she die?"

"Gunshot to the head. Preliminary ruling is a suicide."

"Is that your ruling?" I asked.

"Nothing certain yet, but looks that way to me. 'Course, I haven't really dug into it. Have to go back up later today with some county lab boys. She had the gun in her hand. That's for sure. Saw that with my own eyes. Powder burns on her temple, too. What was left of it."

I shuddered and sank deeper into the safe, warm, secure world of flannel and goose-down feathers. "Poor girl. When did it happen?"

"Can't hear you, Jess. You sound like you're under water."

"Sorry. I'm under the covers. When did it happen?"

"Couple of hours ago. I got the call about one-thirty. Someone found her lying on the floor in her room. Heard the gunshot, they said. I got there right away. Back in my office now. No sense goin' home. The sun'll be up soon."

"Yes. I suppose it will. I'm exhausted. I need a few more hours sleep. How about meeting for breakfast at Mara's?"

He chuckled. "It'll be lunchtime for me," he said.

"So order lunch. Mara will make a hamburger any hour of the day. Seven-thirty? I'd like to hear more about what happened, but I'd also like to be awake enough to fathom what you're saying. Seven-thirty?"

"I'll be there."

By the time I was ready to leave to meet Mort at Cabot Cove's breakfast version of *Cheers,* my phone had rung off the hook. So much for catching a few hours extra sleep.

Most of the calls were from "early-to-bed-early-to-rise" friends who'd caught the early edition of the news on radio. They all wanted to know what I thought of the girl's suicide.

"I don't know any more than you do" was my reply.

Did I think it *was* suicide?

"I don't know."

The conversations didn't last long because I had little to offer. I suppose people assume that a writer of murder mysteries has a sixth sense about death. A secret pipeline to inside sources of information. I don't, which disappoints a lot of people.

The one call that morning that *I* brought to a hasty conclusion was from our mayor, Sybil Stewart.

"You've heard, of course" was how she began.

"Heard what?" I wasn't about to give her the satisfaction of not having to explain herself.

"The death at Worrell. Surely, you've—"

"I heard."

"Shameless. But I suppose it was inevitable. Even I didn't think it would happen so soon."

"I have to run, Sybil."

"I hate to say this, Jess, but I—"

"You told me so."

"Exactly."

"But I don't recall you forecasting that an unfortunate young woman would take her life."

"If she did."

"The gun was in her hand. There were powder burns on her temple."

"It was? There were? How did you—?"

"Have to run, Sybil. Late for a date. Thanks for calling."

"Jessica, how did you—?"

I placed the phone in its cradle, checked my hair one more time in the hall mirror, and headed for Mara's.

As I walked toward the harbor, I couldn't help but reflect on how peaceful Cabot Cove has always been. Although it's grown over the years as more people fall in love with its physical beauty and slower pace, and opt to move here, it remains a community relatively free of violence. We've had our murders. One, maybe two a year. Usually domestic violence, with alcohol involved. There are drugs, of course, but nothing like the big cities. As far as I know, there hasn't been a drug-related murder in Cabot Cove, although that isn't to say it won't happen one day.

There haven't been many suicides in Cabot Cove, either. An old woman who once lived next door to me, and who suffered from a painful terminal disease, took her own life one night. Only a few people were critical of her action. She'd found the peace she needed, and deserved.

The suicide of a teenager a few years ago was more shocking, as might be expected. The town still suffers a communal guilt; could anyone have seen the signs that led to it, and done something to intervene? Probably not, but you do wonder about such things.

In a sense, the death of this young musician at the Worrell Institute for Creativity was removed from Cabot Cove. It hadn't been a townsperson, someone we'd gotten to know over the years. No different, really, than someone who'd checked in for a weekend stay at a local motel.

Or *was* it different?

By the time I walked through the door to Mara's Luncheonette, I'd decided that this death might, indeed, be different. The institute had opened amidst considerable controversy. The people who would come as paying guests were "special" in the sense that they were creative artists, sensitive one would assume, perhaps high-strung, emotionally complex. And possibly tormented, as some artists are when they find it impossible to translate creative thoughts to paper, or to canvas, or to express their inner musical visions.

Maybe the fact that the death at Worrell might not be "just another suicide" was the reason Mort had sounded upbeat on the phone. Every law enforcement officer thrives on controversy and challenge. Like soldiers who need a war, as unfortunate as that reality might be.

Mort hadn't arrived yet; I hoped something hadn't occurred to keep him from showing up. Mara poured me a cup of coffee, and smiled when I reached for a little plastic container of half-and-half that swam in melted ice cubes in an empty margarine container. I'd been trying to develop a taste for skim milk in my coffee, but that experiment had lasted only a week. I try to watch what I eat, but there are certain things that simply don't work, no matter how healthy they might be. Like skim milk in coffee. "Don't say a word, Mara," I said, laughing.

Her smile widened. "I wondered how long you'd last with the skim milk routine. Like drinking gray dishwater, isn't it?"

"Worse."

"Meeting someone?"

"Mort."

"Our fearless sheriff? Haven't seen him. Suppose he's up at Worrell investigating the murder."

"Murder?"

"You didn't hear?"

"No. I mean, I heard about the young musician dying last night, but it was a suicide. Wasn't it?"

"Suicide? Hell, no." The proclamation came from Josh Morgan, owner of Cabot Cove's biggest hardware store, and a vocal foe of the institute since it was first announced. "Somebody shot her right in the head, way's I hear it. Figures."

I ordered blueberry pancakes, and was in the process of cutting them into small pieces in preparation for adding syrup when Mort walked through the door and took a stool next to me. "Still doin' it that way?" he asked.

"Cutting my pancakes before the syrup? Of course. It creates lots of edges to soak up the syrup."

The "art" of eating pancakes had generated considerable debate at Mara's over the years. There was the contingent that considered cutting them first to violate some sacred culinary trust. I belonged to what I preferred to think was the more practical school.

"Hamburger, well-done," Mort told Mara. "Fry up some onions, too."

"Got a suspect yet?" Josh Morgan asked Mort.

"Suspect? No suspect in a suicide."

Morgan guffawed. "Suicide? My rear end. Some doped-up crazy got himself mad at something and started shooting. That's the way I hear it."

"That so?" said Mort. His deep sigh eloquently expressed his annoyance.

"I heard it was a famous rock and roll musician," the postmistress said loudly to a companion at a nearby table.

"No, it wasn't," Mort said, spinning on his stool. "It was a young woman who played classical music. On the flute."

The luncheonette was now abuzz with talk of the death at Worrell. A flurry of questions were directed at Mort, who deflected them with noncommittal responses. Eventually, most of the other customers left; Mort was free to eat his burger in peace. "Sorry I was late," he said between bites. "Got sandbagged on the phone by Dr. O'Neill, the director up at Worrell."

"What does he have to say about what happened?" I asked, sliding my last piece of pancake around in a puddle of syrup.

"Kept talking about image. Reputation. Scandal. Said he hopes I'll handle the investigation with discretion. What's he think I'd do, call a press conference? Go on the Oprah Show?"

I shook my head. "I don't think you'd do that. Anything new in your investigation?" I asked it in a whisper, leaning close to his ear.

He glanced right and left, said into my ear, "No."

"Nothing?"

Another series of looks to ensure we weren't being overheard. "We're calling it a suicide—for now, Jess. But—"

"But what?"

"I got my doubts now after goin' back up there."

"Oh? Can you talk about your doubts?"

"Suppose I shouldn't. But considering it's you—"

I waited.

"Somethin' wrong with the way the gun was in her hand."

My arched eyebrows invited more.

"Too loose. Usually, when somebody shoots themselves, their hand tightens up real tight on the weapon. Can't hardly pry it outta their hand. People who shoot somebody, then try to put the gun in their hand to make it look like suicide, never can get the hand to tighten up. Her hand wasn't tight on the gun."

"What kind of gun was it?" I asked.

"Twenty-two handgun."

"You said there were powder burns on the skin."

"Yup. On the outside. On the skin. Can't tell if there's burns between the skin and bone. Autopsy'll determine that."

"That's important?"

"Sure is. If there's no burn between skin and bone, could mean the gun was held close—but not so close like when somebody holds it to their own head."

"Who's doing the autopsy?"

"Doc Johansen, I assume."

"Hmmmm. Do you know where the girl was from?" I asked.

"California. Los Angeles."

"Has her family been notified?"

"I don't know. Dr. O'Neill said he'd take care of that."

"Was he there when you went to the mansion?"

"No. That's why he called, I guess. Said he arrived right after I left. That doctor with the funny accent—Meti is his name—Dr. Meti was there. Sort of took over things."

"Was he cooperative?" I asked.

"I suppose you could say that. Stayed out of my way at least."

"Did he offer any information about the girl?"

"No. But O'Neill did when he called. Said she was having trouble with her work. Was depressed over how it was going. Some sort of thing she was writing. A musical composition."

"How long had she been at the institute?" I asked

"Couple of weeks, according to O'Neill."

"Was she in some sort of therapy at the institute? I noticed at the party that there were doors leading to a behavioral sciences office. And there was an office that deals with addictions. Was the young woman high on anything?"

"Not that I know. Dr. Meti said she'd been in her room all day except for a personal meeting with Dr. O'Neill. She apparently went back to her room after that meeting. Skipped dinner in the dining room, according to Meti. I suppose O'Neill was last to see her."

"Well, Mort, I enjoyed our breakfast. Lunch for you. My treat." I paid Mara, and we stepped into the cool, refreshing air. It was a crisp Maine fall day, typically pre-Thanksgiving weather with lots of sunshine, and a cameo appearance from a snowflake or two. A schizophrenic wind blew. It was calm one minute; the next minute the wind howled like a nor'easter.

"I'll be calling Dr. O'Neill," I said. "I have to firm up the seminar I'm teaching first week in December."

"What I told you is between us," Mort said.

"Of course. Thanks for sharing it with me."

"If you and that naturally curious mind of yours runs across anything might be of use to me, you'll pass it along?"

"Count on it."

Mort drove off in his patrol car, and I went to a pay phone at the end of the dock. Dr. O'Neill wasn't in. I was transferred to Beth Anne Portledge, O'Neill's administrative assistant. "I'm sorry, Mrs. Fletcher, but with the tragedy that happened last night, Dr. O'Neill is very busy. So am I, as a matter of fact. The press has gotten wind of it and—"

"I won't keep you," I said. "I was hoping to meet

with Dr. O'Neill today regarding my December seminar."

She exhaled an audible whoosh of air. "I don't know if he'll be free at all today."

"I don't mind taking my chances just stopping by. Say later this afternoon?"

"If you wish." She sounded annoyed.

I walked out on the main dock and marveled at the power of the water as it slammed against boats and wooden pilings. The wind had picked up and now blew more consistently. I pulled my green Barbour jacket and red Scottish plaid scarf closer around me and continued to watch as the boats were rocked in the choppy water, and seagulls flying into the wind were rendered motionless, suspended in midair.

I walked the length of the dock. If I were a painter, I thought, I'd choose to paint in Cabot Cove; its natural beauty would make even a bad painter look good. I thought about how great painters managed to capture the light, the flow and the emotion of a scene in their art. In much the same way I try to do in my writing.

I looked out to sea over churning black water and my senses were overwhelmed. The ocean has always given me a sense of satisfaction rivaled by little else in my life. It trivializes things I take too seriously in my day-to-day living. It rekindles my spirituality. It's these things in life that I too often take for granted: an inconsequential walk along a beach, or through the woods. When I open myself to the potency of nature and its cleansing effect, I'm grateful to be alive. If only the young musician at the institute had chosen to take a walk, instead of her life.

When I arrived at the Worrell Mansion at three that afternoon, the circular drive in front of it was chockablock with cars and vans. The signs on two of the vans indicated they were from broadcast media, a television station from Bangor, the other belonging to one of our two local radio stations. The Cabot Cove *Gazette*'s station wagon was there, too, as was Mort Metzger's sheriff's car.

As I was about to climb the steps to the front door, a swell of people, reporters, a camera crew, and unidentified others filed out.

"What's going on?" I asked Matilda Watson, the *Gazette*'s owner.

"Press conference just ended," she replied, walking quickly by.

I entered the mansion and was immediately confronted by Michael O'Neill, the institute's director.

"Hello," I said.

"Jessica Fletcher. What brings you here? Do we have an appointment?"

"No. I spoke with Ms. Portledge this morning and—"

"She told you to come?"

"No. She was very protective of you and your time. But I said I'd stop by and take a chance. Here I am."

"Not a good time, I'm afraid."

"I can imagine. I understand you held a press conference."

"Not much choice, I'm afraid. It seemed easier to

get it over with in one swipe. I had no idea the press could be so aggressive and demanding."

"Their job."

"I suppose so. Well, now that you're here, we can grab a few minutes together. Come. We'll find some peace and quiet in my office."

I followed his long, purposeful steps up a flight of stairs to a suite at the end of a long corridor. He instructed his secretary to hold all calls, and ushered me inside.

The office was spacious. Two walls were painted a forest green; bold. Dark floor-to-ceiling wood-paneled bookshelves lined the other two. A sliding ladder provided access to the upper shelves. A huge Oriental rug dominated the center of the room. A seating area was formed by a large leather couch and two oversize leather wing chairs. Lighting was indirect and flattering. The soft strains of Vivaldi came from unseen speakers.

"Have a seat, Jessica. Coffee? Tea? Something stronger? I have some red zinfandel that's quite nice."

"Nothing, thank you, Doctor."

"Michael. Remember?"

"Yes. Michael."

"Mind if I have something? Strictly for medicinal purposes." He laughed. "An old joke, but apropos. It's been an anxious day, and night."

"Please. Go ahead."

He poured himself what I assumed was brandy into a snifter, inhaled its fumes, then sipped, smacked his lips. "Excellent." He sat in a high-backed leather chair behind his leather inlaid desk and smiled. "Now. I assume you want to discuss your December seminar."

"Yes. Any idea why this young woman took her life?"

His smile turned to laughter. "I have a feeling, Jessica, that you're more interested in what happened here last night than you are in December and seminars."

"If you'd rather not—"

"Professional interest? Plot for your next bestselling book?"

"Absolutely not. Just curious."

He nodded, sipped, placed the snifter on a fabric coaster, and propped his feet on the edge of the desk. "A tragic occurrence, Jessica. Ms. Beaumont had so much to live for. She was beautiful, talented, and well liked. On the surface, she had it all. But inside, she was possessed with an extremely fragile ego. Almost nonexistent. There seemed to be little in her life that mattered except her music. The composition she came here to complete seemed to elude her each day, and she became more despondent. We tried to boost her self-esteem, give her the resolve to finish the work. She was particularly upset that others her age, musicians and composers she knew, were ahead of her in terms of creative output. We did everything we could to help her put things in a more realistic perspective. Obviously, we failed."

"She'd been in therapy with your staff?"

"We don't offer therapy in the traditional sense, Jessica. Did we work with her as a therapist might? Of course."

"Dr. Meti?"

He frowned. "You've met Tomar?"

"Yes. At the party."

"He worked with her. So did I. I had a session with her shortly before she took her life."

"A therapeutic session?"

"If you insist."

I decided I'd asked enough questions about the death, and was about to shift the conversation to my upcoming seminar, but O'Neill stayed with the suicide. "This may sound callous to you, Jessica, but I don't intend it to be. We tried everything in the short time she was here—group, role-playing, hypnotherapy, behavior mod. But with someone as fragile and full of self-doubt as she was, even self-hate, there was little that could be done. With such artists, suicide is not uncommon."

"That doesn't sound at all callous to me, Michael."

"Maybe the fact that I view her death in a positive light will."

"Positive light?"

"Not that she took her life. But we can learn from Maureen Beaumont's death. That's one of the missions of the institute: To study the creative process and artist in the hope of breaking through the sort of problems Maureen suffered. There are hundreds of other Maureen Beaumonts. Maybe thousands. Young, talented, promising artists who hate themselves and cannot rise above the demands they, and others, have placed upon them. Hopefully, what we learn from Maureen Beaumont will help ward off other senseless deaths."

His demeanor, and ability to look me straight in the eye throughout his explanation, earned him credibility. On the other hand, there was a coldness that was off-putting. It sounded, well, callous. Maureen Beaumont had been reduced to a guinea pig of sorts, an experiment. Yes, if something could be learned from her unfortunate state of mind and death that would save others, a small good might come from her demise. I didn't want to be too judgmental of O'Neill. Perhaps he hadn't put it as nicely as I would have wanted. He was under stress. A talented young woman had died in the institution of which he was in charge. I gave him the benefit of doubt.

I would have been happy to get off the subject. But he insisted upon staying with it. "Maureen was living under a thick, dark cloud, Jessica. One of the last things she said to me during our session yesterday afternoon was, 'My mind is like a bad neighborhood that I don't want to go into alone.' I suggested she stay out of that neighborhood, that she explore a new one. She said she'd try. Evidently, she didn't try hard enough."

"Her family must be taking it pretty hard," I said.

"They've already made arrangements to have their daughter's body flown back to California for burial. I understand your sheriff, Mr. Metzger, isn't too happy they'll be performing the autopsy out there instead of here."

"Isn't that unusual?" I asked. "I thought the authority for an autopsy would rest with the jurisdiction in which the death took place."

"Not always. California was her home. The wishes of the family are being honored."

"I understand," I said.

"I hate to be rude, Jessica, but I've scheduled a meeting with Ms. Portledge and some of the staff to try and put this tragedy in better perspective. Could we postpone discussing your seminar? Maybe next week, after the dust settles."

"Of course. Sorry to barge in on you this way. I'll call to set up a meeting. Is there anything I can do regarding Ms. Beaumont?"

"No. But thank you for asking. I'll see you out."

"No need. I dropped bread crumbs on our way here. I'll just follow them."

"All right. I think I'll hide here for the few minutes I have before the meeting. Some quiet thought is very much in order."

And to have another drink, I surmised.

As I descended the stairs to the entrance foyer, Mort Metzger was coming through the front door.

"I saw your car," I said. "I didn't know you'd be here."

"Didn't know you'd be here, either, Jess."

"I just met with Dr. O'Neill."

"About the death?"

"Ah—about my seminar. But we did discuss the suicide. Just in passing."

"I'm going back to her room. We're still dusting for prints, and taking photos."

"Can I tag along?"

"Sure." He motioned me into a corner of the foyer. "Want to know what's goin' on?" he asked.

"Always."

"They're shippin' the body out of the state. Back to California."

"I heard."

"Smells, if you ask me."

"Can't you fight it? Legally, I mean?"

"Not if the county prosecutor goes along with it. He has."

We walked down the long, narrow corridor that was familiar to me because of the tour I'd been given by Beth Anne during the party, and stopped at a door with yellow tape across it that read: CRIME SCENE. Mort held up the tape, and I ducked under. He followed.

A white bedspread with small pink flowers had been showered with blood, now darkened with age. The dresser and desk were coated with a layer of white dust used in searching for fingerprints. White masking tape crudely traced the outline of how her body had been positioned on the floor. Dried blood had accumulated in the area where her head had been.

"Who's the man taking notes?" I asked Mort.

"Oh, him? Another psychiatrist from the institute."

The man to whom I'd referred was, I judged, to be in his mid or late thirties. He was handsome despite having facial features that were too small for his head. He wore half-glasses. His jacket was gray tweed, his shirt a blue button-down. He wore a yellow-and-green paisley bow tie.

"Name's Fechter," Mort said. "Donald Fechter."

"Hello," I said, approaching him.

He looked up from his notepad.

"My name is Jessica Fletcher. I'll be teaching a seminar here in December."

"Oh. I'm Dr. Fechter." We shook hands.

"What a terrible thing," I said, nodding at the white tape on the floor.

"Certainly was," he said, making another note on his pad.

"Are you—well, are you in charge of the investigation?" I asked. "I mean, from the institute's perspective?"

"No, ma'am. Just making sure that no one walks out of here with anything."

"You think the police would—?"

"Excuse me." He went to where Mort stood with one of the technicians. "Are you finished?" he asked in a rather unfriendly tone.

"Almost," Mort replied. "I'll let you know when we are." His tone matched Fechter's. The young psychiatrist went to a corner opposite from where I stood, folded his arms across his chest, and watched the proceedings with a scowl.

"That's it," Mort announced a few minutes later. "Let's wrap it up and get out of here."

"You look exhausted," I said as the technicians packed their bags. Mort's bags were beneath his eyes. Stubble on his hollow cheeks added to his look of fatigue.

"Just realized I've been up for too long," he said, rubbing his eyes. "Got to go back to the office, then hit the hay."

We left the building together.

"What's your opinion now?" I asked.

"Hard to say, Jess. Wish the autopsy were being done here in Maine. Doc Johansen's as good as there is. But that's outta my hands, I'm afraid. Unless something comes up I'm not expecting, it'll be suicide on the death certificate. Probably was."

"But what about her hand not being tight on the weapon?"

His voice was heavy. "Got to excuse me, Jess. I'd better get home before I fall on my face."

"By all means."

I was up at six the next morning, and hard at work on my new novel, *Brandy & Bullets,* by seven. I stayed glued to my word processor until one that afternoon, when I spotted the mailman, Jerry Monk, approaching my mailbox. I met him there, and he handed me a bulging bunch of mail secured with a thick rubber band. "Think you win today, Mrs. Fletcher," he said pleasantly.

"Win?"

"Most mail. Little game I play with myself to break the boredom."

I laughed. "Which makes me your least popular person this day."

"Might say that, only it's not true. But you do get a lot of mail. That's for certain."

As I walked through my front door, I heard a woman talking: ". . . He's been very depressed lately, and I was hoping you could keep on eye on him. Just look in on him from time to time to make sure he's okay. Give a call back when you get a chance. I know you're busy and . . ."

"Hello," I shouted into the phone while turning off my answering machine.

"Jess?"

"Yes. I just walked in and—who is this?"

"It's Jill, Jess. Jill Huffaker."

Jill was an old friend who'd moved to Los Angeles five years earlier—Hollywood, actually—with her husband, Norman, a writer who'd sold two of his books to a major film studio, and then accepted a lucrative screenwriting contract. The novels that had been scooped up by a major film studio had been written under one of a few pseudonyms Norman had used over the years: B. K. Praether. They were westerns, but with few of the clichés we associate with that genre. One was called, *The Redemption of Rio Red,* the other, *The Bronze Lady of Bentonville.*

Jill had been active in community theater in Cabot Cove, and had landed a few small parts in films, and on a television series, after moving to L.A. Nothing major, but enough to keep her spirits high about what might become a career to approximate her husband's professional success.

"What a pleasant surprise," I said. "How are you?"

"Fine. You?"

"Good. Norman?"

"Okay. Well, maybe not so okay. That's why I'm calling. He just left for Cabot Cove."

"Wonderful. Business?"

"Yes. Of a sort. He's going to be spending a few

weeks—at least he says it will be only a few weeks—at the new institute that opened there. Worrell."

"Really? I just came from there. We've had a—I'm teaching a seminar in December."

"That should be interesting."

"Yes, it should. I heard you say that Norman's depressed."

"That's right, Jess. He's been suffering for the past few months from a malady you're probably familiar with. Then again, considering how prolific you are, maybe you haven't ever suffered writer's block."

I laughed. "Oh, yes, I have." I thought of the depressed, blocked Maureen Beaumont; the warmth of my house turned chilly.

"I just thought you might be a dear and check in on him now and then. Frankly, I'm worried about Norman. He's been drinking heavily. Put on a lot of weight. More bloat, I guess you could call it. He seems to have lost all his spark, his zest for life."

The room grew colder still.

"Of course I'll keep in touch with him. I'll be going to the institute anyway now and then. I'll just make it more of a regular habit."

"I knew I could count on you, Jess. Working on something new?"

"Yes. Well into a new novel. No writer's block. At least not yet. Any chance of you coming here to visit Norm?"

"Not planning on it, but you never know. I'll let you go. Thanks again. Maybe I will plan to visit. Talking with you makes me realize how much I miss the East Coast, and friends like Jessica Fletcher."

"Don't worry about a thing, Jill. Norman will be in good hands." I winced as I said it. I knew *my* hands would be good. But considering what had happened to the young flautist, I probably shouldn't be issuing such positive statements about the Worrell Institute for Creativity.

Chapter Six

"Make that two pumpkin and one apple," I said, proud that I'd finally made up my mind. Usually, I'm capable of making swift, rational decisions, especially if the dilemma is of some importance. It's over little decisions that I often trip, my mind changing as rapidly and often as New England weather.

Like deciding what pies to order. Give me a murder plot to unravel, and I leave no clue unturned. Ask me how many pies I need for Thanksgiving dinner, and I inevitably arrive at a hung jury.

"No, wait," I said to Charlene Sassi, owner of Cabot Cove's finest fancy food store and bakery. How she could own a bakery and still maintain her pencil-thin figure will always be an enigma to me. "Bear with me for a minute, Charlene. I'm still not sure how many I need."

I looked up at the wood-beamed ceiling from which dozens of pretty wicker baskets hung, closed my eyes, and silently counted once again the number of guests who would be sitting at my round oak table on Thanksgiving Day, one week from today. "Okay, all set," I said. Charlene had waited patiently despite a crush of other customers, hand on her hip, head cocked to the side. "Two apple pies, one pumpkin, and one clam. That'll do it. I think."

"You said you're having seven guests, right?" she said. "Unless they come in extra large sizes, you've ordered more than enough."

"Thanks for your patience. Pick them up Thanksgiving morning? You open at six?"

"Ayuh. Same time, same place, just higher prices. Next?"

My order for holiday pies placed, I headed for lunch with old friend and screenwriter Norman Huffaker. He'd gone straight to the Worrell Institute for Creativity upon arriving in Cabot Cove, and called me that evening. It was good to hear his voice, although he sounded different than the last time we'd talked. But that was over a year ago. I probably sounded different, too.

He wasn't overly enthusiastic about meeting for lunch, but I prevailed. "I promised Jill I'd keep an eye on you," I said lightly, adding a laugh for emphasis. He didn't laugh. I sensed annoyance.

"All right," he said. "Lunch it is. But we'll have to make it a quick one. I came to Worrell to get over this damnable block I'm having. Nothing ever gets written over lunch."

And that's how we left it. I was tempted to call it off. I certainly didn't want to be perceived as having intruded upon his work for something as frivolous as lunch. On the other hand, I wanted to see him. After all, he was an old friend. And—I wasn't at all guilty about this—I wanted to hear what scuttlebutt he might have picked up about Maureen Beaumont's alleged suicide.

I'd chosen for us to meet at a pleasant inn diagonally across the road from Sassi's bakery. The inn's bar and restaurant was called The Office, although it wouldn't be confused with any office I've ever seen. The dining room was warm and inviting, with richly paneled walls on which stunning landscapes and seascapes by local artists were proudly displayed, and were for sale. The many windows were graced with gingham curtains. A walk-in fireplace was used year-round. The tables were large, and tastefully set with quilted placemats, sparkling crystal, and weighty silverware. It had become a favorite meeting place: the dining room for family brunches, tasty lunches, and hearty dinners, and the bar a congenial spot for drinks after work. Everything came under the watchful eye of the inn's owner, Mick Jones, who wore many hats: bartender, host, waiter, and even busboy when the crush was on.

The air was invigoratingly cold as I left Sassi's and headed for the inn. I'd neglected to thoroughly dry my hair that morning and shivered as a chill raced from my head down my spine. A recurrence of last year's pneumonia was not part of my winter agenda, and I hurried across the road and inside the inn. I'd requested the table directly in front of the fireplace when I made the reservation, and it was waiting for me, the advantage of having become a regular customer. I shed my coat and sat in my favorite wooden armchair. The heat from the fireplace warmed my back; I could look out over the dining room. The chair felt like an old friend. Had I sat in it enough to cause it to have adjusted to the curves of my body? Certainly not, but I preferred to think that.

Because I was early, and Norman hadn't arrived yet, I took out my small black leather notebook, scrutinized my "To Do" list, added a few items, and crossed off others. My first stop after lunch would be Zach's Orchard and Farm where I'd order the turkey, and stuffing to which I would add certain ingredients to make it uniquely mine. The grocery store was next on the list: yams, cranberries, potatoes, onions, and makings for what had become my "famous" hard sauce. Charlene's pumpkin and apple pies were fabulous on their own, but adding my hard sauce to them was always, and literally, icing on the cake.

Liquor? Although I'm not much of a drinker, I always keep a fully stocked bar for guests. My only concern was Jill's comment that Norman had taken to heavy drinking. I intended over lunch to invite him to my house for Thanksgiving, and didn't want to exacerbate any problem he might be having with alcohol. On the other hand, I don't believe in penalizing moderate drinkers to accommodate someone with a problem. Norman was a big boy, as they say. My bar would be open. Alexander's Fancy Wine & Spirits was added to the list.

I knew someone had entered the dining room by the sudden blast of cold outside air that preceded the new arrival. Norman closed the door and eyed the room. I stood and waved him to the table.

He walked slowly in my direction, lips pursed, his six feet, four inch frame somewhat bent. He moved slowly, like a man unsure of his destination. He could have been drunk. If he was, his drinking problem was greater than even his wife knew. It was barely noon.

I was heartened when a smile crossed his face as he reached the table. We hugged. "You look fabulous, Jessica," he said. "And please don't feel a need to reciprocate the compliment. I wouldn't want to make a liar out of you."

"You look—fine," I said.

He'd made a liar out of me.

His face was bigger, bloated, and blotchy. His hair was matted, needing a healthy dose of shampoo. I noticed two things as he unbuttoned his topcoat. A button was missing. And, his hands shook. I pretended not to notice.

"Thought you'd appreciate the fireplace," I said, looking into it. "I assume your blood's been thinned by all those glorious sunny days in Hollywood." He politely joined my laughter, and we sat.

"Gets cold in L.A. sometimes," he said absently, his gaze on the fire which illuminated eyes that were, to this observer, glassy. I hadn't smelled alcohol on his breath. But then again I've never had a particularly keen sense of smell. He seemed mesmerized by the flickering flames.

"Norman? Come in, Norman."

He jerked his head toward me. "What?"

"You okay?" I asked.

"Am I—? Okay? Oh, sure. Sorry. Got lost in my thoughts for a moment. Fires do that to me. They suck you in. At least they do me."

"Me, too. Very hypnotic."

He leaned his elbows on the table and said, "Well, Jessica, it's really great to see you. I'm glad we're doing this. And sorry if I came off the oaf when you called. I was tired. Damn time difference. Throws off your circadian rhythm."

"Yes."

"How've you been?" His attention drifted back to the fireplace.

I was tempted to say, "Dying of a dreadful disease, thank you. And you?" just to see if he was listening. I didn't, of course. He was obviously troubled, about what I didn't know. His inability to complete his latest screenplay? If his current mood was the result of so-called writer's block, I could certainly understand, especially with a writer like Norman Huffaker. Although I've always considered myself a productive writer, my yearly output paled in comparison to his. He'd always been impressively prolific, banging out one screenplay after another on any number of subjects—documentaries, comedies, romances, westerns. If that ability to turn thoughts into words on paper had deserted him, I hoped that Worrell would renew his spirit, and return him to productivity.

"Vodka gimlet," he told Clara, our waitress, who'd been serving me since The Office opened three years ago. A glass of sherry was appealing, but I thought of all the shopping I had to do and chose a cup of tea instead.

We chatted about Norman's plane trip to Cabot Cove—the flight had been delayed, adding to the fatigue he felt upon arriving—until his drink was served. He downed it, pointed to the almost empty glass, and told Clara, "Let's do this again." She shot me a raised-eyebrow look and headed for the bar.

"So, Jessica Fletcher, tell me about you." He lit a cigarette despite a nearby NO SMOKING sign, and the absence of an ashtray on the table. "Working on another best-seller?"

"More like putting it off," I said. "My father always said that procrastination was the thief of time. I've been stealing a lot of time lately. I understand you've been doing some of that yourself."

"Says my lovely and adoring wife? My spy? She's right. I've become the world's most adept procrastinator. It's gotten so bad, I've gotten good at putting off entire days of the week. Just this past Monday, I woke up and said, "Not today. I'll do Monday tomorrow. I went back to sleep until Tuesday." He let out a rasping smoker's laugh and coughed. He'd meant the story to be funny, but I didn't take it that way. I'm no shrink. But I do know that one of the signs of serious depression can be to pull the covers over one's head in the hope the world will go away.

"Sorry, sir, no smoking," Clara said when she returned with his second drink. "Smoking in the bar only."

Norman took it better than I anticipated. He's always been a heavy smoker; the recent frenzied antismoking campaign, which even I as a nonsmoker feel has gone too far, evidently hadn't had its intended impact upon him.

"Want to move to a table in the bar?" I asked.

"Nah. I just hope we're not sitting in the

anticholesterol section." He smiled, took two more puffs, and went to the bar to extinguish his cigarette.

"How are things going at Worrell?" I asked when he returned.

"Pretty good, considering a gal there recently killed herself. Shook everybody up pretty bad. I assume you know about it."

"I certainly do."

"Was it really a suicide, Jess?"

"As far as I know. That's what they're saying."

"You still have that same sheriff in Cabot Cove? Metzger?"

"Yes. Morton Metzger is still the sheriff."

"What's *he* say?"

"Uh, suicide, I think." Mort hadn't seemed so sure the last time we spoke. I wondered what his latest thoughts were.

"Casts an eerie glow over the institute, doesn't it?" Norman said, pulling his cigarettes from his pocket, smiling, and putting them back. "Ironic. Here I am trying to get over a terminal case of writer's block, and somebody in the room next to mine blows her brains out. I guess she got over *her* block, whatever the hell it was. Maybe that's the real answer."

"I don't think it's the answer to anything, Norm. I can understand how difficult it might be to write with the aura of death hanging over the premises. Hardly an atmosphere conducive to writing."

"Unless, of course, you're writing a murder mystery."

"*Murder* mystery? Why do you say that?"

"I don't know. Sure I can't smoke here? You're a VIP. Pull rank."

"Sorry. Can't do. Why did you say murder?"

"Maybe she didn't pull the trigger."

"Anything to back that up?"

"Nope. I leave that to you."

"Thank you."

"Have you ever had writer's block, Jessica?"

I thought about it for a minute.

"If you have to think about it, you never have. It's not the kind of thing you easily forget."

"I suppose I never have. I have days, even a week, when my writing isn't at its best. But I can't say I've ever had a period longer than a week when I wasn't able to write—well. Jill said you've been having quite a time with it. Months?"

"Feels a lot longer than that," he said. "I'm trying to finish a screenplay I've been working on for two years."

"What's it about?" I asked.

"Takes place in the 'Thirties. In Hollywood."

"A *Sunset Boulevard* story?"

"No. I forget what it's about, it's been so long that I've worked on it." He laughed. It was reassuring he could laugh about his problems.

"Jessica, do you think this young woman, Maureen Beaumont, might have been murdered?" He obviously preferred to talk about that instead of his work—or anything else, for that matter.

"I have no evidence to suggest that, Norm. But Sheriff Metzger is very capable. He's directed the investigation at the institute and seems to be on top of things. And he's a good friend. He'll keep me up-to-date, I'm sure. Of course, he is concerned about—"

"Concerned about what?"

"I suppose there's no reason you shouldn't know. It's been in the paper. Ms. Beaumont's body was immediately flown back to California. Family's request. Morton would have preferred that the autopsy be done here."

"Sure. It should have been done here."

"She was from Los Angeles. Silly question, I know, but did you know her?"

"Silly question. Four thousand square miles, eight million people."

"Not like Cabot Cove."

"*Nothing* like Cabot Cove. Metzger, the sheriff. Did he say that—?"

"Ask him yourself."

The door had opened, and Mort was swept in on a blast of frigid air. He walked with purpose, straight to our table. "Sorry to interrupt your lunch, Jess."

"That's all right, Mort," I said. "We haven't gotten to lunch yet. This is—"

"Can we talk?"

His lack of manners in not acknowledging Norman was off-putting. It also told me that something serious was on his mind.

"This is Norman Huffaker, Mort. Maybe you remember him. He and his wife, Jill, lived in Cabot Cove a number of years ago."

"Nice to meet you," Mort said, extending his hand. "Jess?"

"Sit down," I said. "I'm sure whatever you want to tell me can be said in front of Norman."

Norman got up. "You two chat," he said. "Time for a cigarette anyway." I watched him carry his drink to the empty bar, order another from the owner, Mick, and light up. Mort took Norman's chair.

"How did you know I'd be here?" I asked.

"Joyce, down at the post office, said you'd been in, and were heading for Charles's Department Store to buy Christmas wrapping paper. David, there, said you told him you were goin' to Sassi's. Charlene told me—"

"I get the picture," I said. "The Cabot Cove grapevine in full gear."

Morton leaned close. "Jess, Worrell is starting to look more like Jonestown every day."

"Jonestown? Oh, where all those unfortunate people followed that crazed preacher and killed themselves. Why do you say that?" I'd already surmised the answer.

"Another young woman was taken to the hospital in the middle of the night. Attempted suicide, they're saying."

"*Attempted* suicide. She's alive?"

"Barely. In ICU. Seth was there when they brought her in. Been with her ever since."

"That's why I couldn't reach him this morning. Know anything about her?"

"A poet, they say."

"A gunshot wound?"

"No. Some sort of pills. They pumped her stomach over to the hospital, sent the contents out for analysis. Poor girl was evidently unconscious for quite a spell before anybody found her. Seth says her brain was without oxygen a long time. If she lives, might not be much more than a vegetable."

"Horrible."

I looked to where Norman drank, smoked, and talked with Mick. He was at Worrell last night? Didn't he know about this latest incident? If he did, why hadn't he mentioned it to me?

I said to Mort, "My friend over there, Norman Huffaker, checked into Worrell a few days ago. He was there last night. You'd think that—"

"Most people probably don't even know it happened. The young woman lived in one of the cottages on the estate. Pretty far removed from the main house."

"How was she found?" I asked.

"A friend stopped in to see her. Found her comatose in bed."

"Have you examined the room?"

"Nope. Police weren't called, at least by anybody at Worrell. Got the call from Seth at the hospital. I called Ms. Portledge and woke her up. She confirmed what happened. Overdose of pills, she told me."

"Any idea why she tried to kill herself?"

"I asked Ms. Portledge that. She says this gal was close with Maureen Beaumont. Pretty upset over what happened to her friend."

I again looked to where Norm sat at the bar. I was content to continue my conversation with Mort, but was afraid that if it went on too long, Norman would become falling-down drunk.

"Keep this between us, Jess," Mort said.

"Why? It'll be all over town by the end of the day."

"I know that. Didn't realize your friend was at Worrell. I seem to remember him now. Real pretty wife. He was a writer."

"Still is. Hollywood. Motion pictures."

"One of them, huh?"

I didn't challenge his snap appraisal of Norman.

"You're right, Jess. Everybody'll know. But what you and me can keep between us is that from this day forward, the Worrell Institute for Craziness is under investigation by this sheriff and his office. Too much of a damn coincidence havin' two people try to kill themselves up there. I don't want anybody up there—O'Neill, Portledge, any of the shrinks—to know I'll be keeping close tabs on them from now on."

"Your secret is safe with me, Mort."

"If I didn't think it was, Jess, I wouldn't have told you. Got to go. Thanks for lettin' me barge in like this. Say goodbye to your friend."

Norm returned to the table, a fresh drink in his hand. I didn't know how many drinks he'd had, but they didn't seem to have had much of an effect on him. "Trouble?" he asked.

"No. Hungry?"

"Yes."

"They make a wonderful beef stew," I said.

"Sounds good."

I gave Clara the order. "Norm, did you know that someone else at Worrell tried to kill herself last night?"

"No." His red face turned ashen. He put his drink down and rubbed his eyes.

"Norm. Are you okay?"

"What was her name?" he asked.

"I don't know. Mort didn't mention it."

"I've got to go, Jess. I forgot I have a meeting at Worrell this afternoon."

I didn't believe him for a moment.

"Sorry." He motioned Clara to the table. "Put a stop on that second beef stew," he said. "And give me the check. I have to run."

Clara looked quizzically at me before heading for the kitchen. "Norm," I said. "Is there something wrong? Did my mentioning this latest tragedy upset you?"

"Of course not. We'll do this again soon." He put on his coat as Clara laid the check on the table.

"Norm, I'd love it if you would come for Thanksgiving dinner next week. I'll be making my hard sauce. Please come."

"Sure, that would be great, Jess." He laid money on the check, kissed my cheek, and headed for the door.

"What was that all about?" Clara asked.

"I have no idea. But I'd like to know."

"If you find out, Jess, let me know, too. Never seen anybody scoot outta here so fast. Still want your stew?"

"Yes, please. I always get hungry when I've been abandoned at a table."

As usual, the beef stew was excellent, but my mind wasn't on food. Obviously, my mention of this latest suicide attempt at Worrell had upset Norm enormously, sent him scurrying away. Why? It couldn't have been that he knew the victim, because I hadn't mentioned any name. Strange. Would he show up for Thanksgiving? I doubted it. But I resolved not to let him off the hook too easily. I'd keep in touch and remind him of it. I wanted him there more than ever.

Clara brought me a glass of brandy after lunch.

"You have the wrong table," I said.

"No, I don't, Jess. Your friend told me on his way out the door to bring this to you."

I took a sip from the fat snifter and turned my face toward the fire. Should I call Jill and tell her of Norm's unusual behavior? I decided not to. Maybe he did have a meeting he'd forgotten about. Maybe he suddenly wasn't feeling well and didn't want to worry me. Maybe . . .

I hate maybes.

I ran all the errands on my lists despite the sleepiness the brandy had induced, and was happy to return home where I made a cup of strong tea, and munched on a cranberry cookie Charlene Sassi had insisted I put in my purse.

There were several messages on my answering machine. One caught my attention for two reasons: It was from a person I hadn't seen or talked to for quite a while; and, it was an invitation I immediately decided to accept.

I'd met Carson James on a flight between Chicago and Houston. I was on tour promoting a book, and he was on his way to appear in a Houston nightclub. Carson is a stage hypnotist, a performer.

We kept in touch on an irregular basis. Although he'd invited me on many occasions to catch his act, it never worked out. We fell out of touch about two years ago. But here he was. He said on my machine's tape:

"Hello there my dear. This is your ghost from Christmas past. Wonderful to hear your voice again, even though it's recorded and distorted. You really should have the machine checked. Poor quality. I call to report that following a two-year hiatus, during which I served my country in the Peace Corps—I'll fill you in on that later—I'm alive and well and living in Boston. I'm also back on the nightclub circuit, and am performing this weekend at a charming little dive here in Boston called Tickletoes. I insist that you be my guest, Jessica, and will not accept a negative reply. And please feel free to bring a friend, or some significant other. It won't cost you anything, except, of course, getting to Boston, hotel, and other incidentals of traveling, which, I know, you are intimately familiar with. I trust this message finds you well. I look forward to speaking with you, and to seeing you once again. Ta ta for now. Oh, by the way, my new number is 617-555-3553."

It was the perfect weekend to go to Boston. I hadn't been there for some time, and Seth had mentioned he was planning to go in the next couple of weeks to do some Christmas shopping. My Thanksgiving shopping was basically completed. I'd shelved working on my book. The weekend was free of social obligations.

Yes. I would go, and encourage Seth to go with me.

There was another reason for deciding to head for Boston and this "charming little dive" called Tickletoes. I've always been fascinated with hypnosis. Although I've never been a subject of it—I was told I wouldn't be a good one—I delved into it a number of years ago as background for a novel in which hypnosis played a role in the resolution of the plot. I consulted with doctors known for their use of it in medical situations, and walked away from the learning experience impressed and excited about my newfound knowledge. It would be fun to see a professional practice hypnosis, even in a nightclub setting.

And, I reminded myself as I went through the process of convincing myself to take Carson James up on his offer, that hypnosis was part of the package offered at the Worrell Institute for Creativity. A refresher course couldn't hurt.

Carson sounded sincerely pleased when I reached him and said I would be there for his Saturday night show, and that Seth had agreed to accompany me. Carson's only reservation, which he proclaimed in his theatrical, overblown fashion, was that many doctors look upon stage hypnotists with scorn.

"Not this doctor," I quickly told him. "The only thing Seth scorns are people who are scornful. See you Saturday."

Chapter Seven

The only problem in going away with Seth Hazlitt is that he's the quintessential early-morning person. He's always up at the crack of dawn, showered, shaved, and breakfasted by six, jolly and alert, excited about what the day might bring. I respect that. But leaving for Boston at five A.M. Saturday morning "in order to beat the traffic" seemed a bit much.

"Could we leave at six?" I asked, thinking I'd offered a reasonable alternative.

"By six, Jessica, everybody and his brother'll be on the road. Be at your house at five sharp."

We were Boston-bound at 5:05.

I love Boston, always have. I've stayed at a number of fine hotels there, but the Bostonian has become a particular favorite of late. Despite its central location—just across from Faneuil Hall and the bustling Quincy Market—it has the quiet charm of a small, secluded European retreat, with its cobblestone courtyard entrance, sedate lobby, and tastefully furnished and decorated rooms. I believe in indulging myself in a hotel's better rooms when traveling. Once I've committed to the cost of staying at a hotel, the few extra dollars to upgrade seem worth it. I'd reserved a room with a fireplace and with a balcony that afforded a wonderful view of the market. Seth doesn't share my enthusiasm for a touch of opulence when traveling. I reserved the smallest, least expensive room for him, on his instructions.

Although it wasn't yet Thanksgiving, the holiday season was in full swing in Boston that day, as shoppers braved a brisk, cold wind in search of the perfect early Christmas gift. Seth and I were swept up in the spirit, and I returned to the hotel delighted that I'd gotten such an impressive start on my list. I was also exhausted. Carson James had told me that Tickletoes was a comedy club catering to the younger set, which meant the entertainment started late, and ended even later. The first show was at nine-thirty. It was now five-thirty. Seth and I had agreed to meet for dinner at Seasons, the hotel's fourth-floor restaurant, at seven. That left me an hour and a half to sink into my room's Jacuzzi, relax in front of a fire—undoubtedly to doze a bit—then dress and head out for the evening.

We took a cab to the comedy club because Seth decided the neighborhood in which it was located, on the fringe of Boston's notorious "Combat Zone," wasn't a safe place to park his Toyota. It was a good thing Carson had reserved a table for us, because when we arrived, there was a block-long line outside Tickletoes.

We were spirited to a table directly in front of the tiny stage and microphone. I glanced about. There were a few people our age, but not many. You could tell who they were without having to see their faces because they were dressed like us—suits and ties for the men, dresses on the women. Everyone else wore a uniform of sorts—jeans, sweaters, and an astounding number of baseball hats, most of them worn backward.

"Never will understand wearin' hats indoors," Seth muttered as a young waitress delivered our drinks. "Bad manners."

"It's the style," I said.

"Ayuh, I know that. Still doesn't excuse bad manners."

"Cheers," I said. We clinked rims.

"Jessica!"

I looked up at a smiling Carson James. Seth started to stand, but James placed a hand on his shoulder. "No need for formality, my good man," he said. There was a third chair at the table, which James took. He looked much as he had the last time I'd seen him. Carson James was very tall, and very thin. The elongation of his face was exaggerated by a pointy, black Vandyke beard hanging like a black icicle from his chin. Hair on his head was sparse, a few wet black strands pasted from front to back. He wore steel-rimmed glasses, which framed unusually small eyes, little black beads that seemed incapable of resting on anything.

I introduced Seth to Carson, and they shook hands. "A medical doctor," James said loudly. "My medical career was thwarted in midstream. Lack of money."

"I'm sorry," Seth said.

"And, I'll be candid, a lifelong abhorrence of blood. Mine, or anyone else's."

We laughed. "A distinct disadvantage," said Seth.

"Do you use hypnosis in your practice?" James asked Seth.

"Ayuh. Now and then. Help a smoker kick the habit, help an insomniac get some sleep." I was pleased that Seth didn't dismiss Carson's specialty. He's always been skeptical of hypnosis, despite using it in special situations. But then he added, "Don't have much faith in it, 'cept for certain types of people."

"I'm excited to finally see you perform, Carson," I said quickly. "All these years gone by."

"I'll make it an extra special evening for you, dear lady." He kissed my hand. "Time for me to be backstage. I hope you enjoy the show, Doctor."

"I'm sure I will," Seth said.

It occurred to me that dragging Seth along might not have been my best idea. He was not a man who enjoyed nightclubs and comedians. Add hypnosis to that mix and it was unlikely he'd find the experience uplifting. But too late for that now. Even if he hated it, he'd be gracious about it, one of many traits I've always admired in my friend.

We declined a second drink as the house lights dimmed, a single spotlight illuminated the microphone, and a cherubic young man wearing "the uniform" bounced on to the stage. "Hey, hey, how are we tonight?" he boomed. The audience erupted in whistles and applause. "Welcome to Tickletoes. Have we got a lineup for you tonight." He ran off some names before saying, "And Boston's own mesmerizing Carson James is with us."

"Awright!!"

"Lets get it on!"

The enthusiasm was catching. I couldn't help but laugh. Poor Seth. The best he could manage was to avoid grimacing.

Carson James was the featured attraction that night, which meant sitting through a half-dozen young men and women telling jokes. A few were funny; all were dirty, although I suspected their generation of fans found nothing salacious about them.

Finally, the MC announced Carson, who ambled to the mike and waved to the audience. He wore a black dinner jacket with silver sequins, and a red bow tie. Six straight-back chairs were lined up behind him. He looked down at me. "We have a real live celebrity in the audience tonight," he said.

I wanted to crawl under the table.

"My friend, and the world's greatest mystery writer, Jessica Fletcher. Stand up, Jess. Take a bow."

I rose an inch off my chair, and nodded.

James pointed to a young woman at the table next to us, then to a man, another woman, and three others. "Come up here," he commanded. After much giggling, and a few vocal protestations, they all did, to my surprise

Carson had them sit facing us in the chairs. He snapped his fingers: "You're going into a trance, a deep and relaxing state of mind. Deeper. Deeper. Close your eyes. You can't keep your eyes open. Your eyelids are heavy. Heavy. It feels so good to close your eyes and to float to pleasant places. Your body feels as though there are helium-filled balloons attached to it, making you feel light. Lighter. Lighter. Buoyant. Floating. You're so relaxed, carefree, floating, floating, hearing only my voice. Only me. My voice. Deeper. Deeper. Lighter. Lighter. More buoyant."

Carson tossed out occasional humorous asides to the audience, which resulted in a few laughs. But the mood in the small room had become quiet, serious. Everyone, including Seth and I, leaned closer to the stage and watched with fascination as Carson continued to hypnotize his subjects.

Carson focused on one of the young women, who seemed to have been most affected by his hypnotic instructions. She sat placidly, her eyes closed, arms dangling loosely at her sides, a smile on her face. Carson touched her forehead and said, "Your left arm is light and buoyant. Let it float up." Her arm slowly ascended. "That's right," Carson said. "Now, I want you to stand." She got up. "The sun is shining brightly," he said. "The barnyard is a warm and happy place—and you're a happy little chicken."

Snickers from the audience.

"Listen to me," Carson said. "You're going deeper, deeper, deeper into your pleasant trance. And you hear only me, my voice. Go ahead and speak like a chicken. I'm speaking to you. You have something to say."

The young woman started clucking.

"And you want to fly. Go ahead. Flap your wings." She tucked her hands beneath her armpits, and energetically moved her elbows up and down, accompanied by her clucking.

Carson told her she could stop, and had her sit down. He went to another subject, a young man with a baseball hat on backward, and had him stand. Within a few minutes, this person was doing crude ballet dance steps, much to the delight of the audience, now very much into what Carson was accomplishing onstage.

He didn't attempt to have all six subjects act silly. He worked with only four of them, allowing the remaining two to be bystanders to the others's antics.

As Carson was about to bring everyone out of their respective trances, he instructed them that they would remember nothing of what had transpired on the stage, but that when they heard the song, "When Johnny Comes Marching Home," they would again become a chicken, a ballet dancer, and the roles Carson had given the others to perform.

"Awake!" Carson commanded, snapping his fingers.

The six subjects came to attention, opened their eyes, smiled, then laughed, and took their seats in the audience.

"Amazing," I said to Seth over the lingering applause.

"Plants in the audience," he said.

"Oh, no, Seth. I don't think so."

Carson took the microphone. "They say writers go into a sort of trance state when they write," he said. "They lose themselves in the scenes and characters they create." He looked down at me. "Am I right, Jessica?"

I shrugged.

"Come up here." He motioned with his index finger for me to join him onstage.

"Oh, no," I said.

"Please," Carson said. "Just a friendly little experiment in the interest of science."

I looked to Seth, whose expression said I should accommodate Carson. It wasn't what I wanted to see. I wanted Seth to shake his head, which would have given me the resolve to decline. But Seth hadn't given me that sign, and Carson was still motioning, so I stood, straightened my dress, and climbed up next to him. The applause was loud.

"Ever see the world's greatest mystery writer go into a trance?" he asked the audience.

"Do it!" someone yelled.

"Awright!!"

"Carson, I really don't think I should—"

"Relax, Jessica. Close your eyes. Think of pleasant thoughts. A beach at sunset. Relax. Relax. That's right. Think of your lovely home in Maine. A fire burning. Warm. Comfortable. Just hear me. Your eyes are closed because your eyelids are heavy. Very, very heavy. That's right. Your left arm is attached to helium-filled balloons and wants to float up over your head. Lighter and lighter. Let it go, Jess. Let it float free."

I can only report in retrospect what I felt during the time with Carson James on that small stage. It was blissful. I was totally relaxed, felt light as a feather. Seth told me later that I had a wide smile on my face throughout, until—

Until Carson had me sit in a chair. "You're driving down a beautiful coastline, Jessica," he said.

That's when, according to Seth, my smile changed to a frown, and then a panicked look crossed my face. Carson saw the change, too, and asked if I was feeling all right.

"She doesn't drive," Seth hissed from the audience.

My arms stretched in front of me, and my right foot tapped the floor in search of a brake pedal. Carson quickly brought me out of my trance, thanked me, and I returned to the table.

"You looked right petrified up there," Seth said.

"I was driving a car, Seth. I was afraid because I didn't know how to stop it. I thought I was going to plunge over a ledge."

"Damn fool thing for him to be doin' to people," Seth said.

"Well, it's over," I said.

Carson ended his act by whistling the first few bars of "When Johnny Comes Marching Home" into the microphone. The people at surrounding tables who'd been his earlier subjects went into their crazy routines again, a chicken clucking and flapping her elbows, the young man with the baseball hat standing, his arms extended above his head in a circle as he attempted an intricate ballet move. Carson brought them back to the stage, told them everything he'd said would now be forgotten, and that hearing that particular song would no longer mean anything to them. He took his bows and strode from the stage.

Minutes later he was at our table. He took my hand in his and said, "I'm sorry, Jessica. It never dawned on me that you didn't drive."

"That's all right," I said. "But I must admit there was a moment there when I was frightened. Incredible, how you actually had me in a car. I wasn't here in this club. I was in a car, behind the wheel."

"Dangerous thing you do, Mr. James," Seth said sternly.

"Not really, Doctor. What happened to Jessica doesn't happen often. The moment I saw that she was in some sort of distress, I brought her right out of it."

"Maybe that's 'cause Jess is a strong woman. What happens when you get somebody who's a perfect subject for hypnosis, a 'five' on the Spiegel scale of hypnotizability?"

"You're familiar with Dr. Spiegel's Hypnotic Induction Profile?" Carson said.

"Ayuh. Took a course once with him down at Columbia Presbyterian Hospital in New York City. Learned a lot."

Two people came to the table and asked me for my autograph, which I happily gave them.

I said to Seth, "I didn't realize you knew as much as you do about hypnosis."

"I don't know much, 'cept that everything depends on the subject. Some folks are good, some not so good. You can do damn near anything with a good subject, one of those 'fives' I mentioned." He looked at Carson James. "Am I right?"

"Yes. Well, you really can't do *anything* with such a person."

"You can't?" I said. "I thought—"

Carson smiled. "I have a splendid idea," he said. "It's an hour before my next show. I know a fine little pub a block from here. What say we retire there for a much-deserved nightcap for Jessica, and continue this conversation?"

"Seth?" I asked.

"Fine with me," he said. "Need a check."

"Absolutely not," Carson said. "My treat. Part of my deal with Tickletoes is that I get to entertain two guests at each show. You're my two guests at this one. Come, I'd like to pick the doctor's considerable brain about this thing I do for a living on the stages of the world."

The pub was called Boston Beans. It was a small neighborhood place with a fireplace, and country-and-western music on the jukebox. We took a booth near the door. Seth and I each had a brandy, Carson a vodka martini, straight up. I resumed the conversation where it had ended at Tickletoes.

"I thought you could make people do things under hypnosis that are uncharacteristic of their basic nature," I said.

"Not true, my dear Jessica," Carson said, tasting his drink and pronouncing it satisfactory with a loud smack of his lips. Seth sat quietly and listened as Carson explained. "You see, no matter how skilled the hypnotist, or good the subject, people will not do something that violates their moral code." He laughed. "You've heard about those teenage boys with the fantasy that they can hypnotize a young lady, and convince her to disrobe in their presence. Impossible! Unless, of course, she is the sort of young lady whose moral code does not preclude such behavior. Am I right, Dr. Hazlitt?"

"Yes. And no."

I raised my eyebrows at Seth. "Not your usual filled-with-conviction response to a question."

"Mr. James here is basically right," said Seth. "But people can be made to act contrary to their deep beliefs if the hypnotist, working with a very good subject, changes the visual."

"What does that mean?" I asked.

Seth explained: "One example is what Mr. James has raised, that of the common teenage male fantasy that a girl can be induced to disrobe. A hypnotist can't command her to do that. But a skilled hypnotist might be able to convince this same young lady that she is alone in a room, and that the temperature of that room has become unbearably hot. Given that scenario, she might well remove her clothes."

"Esterbrooks," James said.

"Among others. A book, *The Control of Candy Jones,* explains it as well as any I've read. I have a copy, Jessica. Happy to lend it to you."

"I'll look forward to it. She was the famous model."

"Among other things, including a CIA experimental guinea pig. Let me take it a step further," Seth said. "A hypnotist would have a difficult, probably impossible time convincing even the best of subjects to shoot his wife—provided he loves her, of course, and is not a basically violent man. But again, by changing the visual, it could be done. The subject—and again I stress it must be a good subject, a 'five' on the Spiegel scale—could be convinced that when his wife walks through the door of his home, it isn't his wife at all, but a hungry, rabid bear. He must shoot it in self-defense."

"I see," I said. "Fascinating."

"Your physician friend is astute and knowledgeable," Carson James said.

"About many things," I said. "Carson, I now understand how people can be tested to determine their hypnotizability. This Hypnotic Induction Profile you both seem to know so much about. But you didn't test the subjects you brought to the stage tonight. Or did you? Did you know them before the show, have an opportunity to find who would be your best subjects?"

Carson laughed. "You mean were they 'plants,' shills for my act? Heavens, no, Jessica. That would be cheating." He looked to Seth. "Wouldn't it, Doctor Hazlitt?"

"Ayuh. That it would."

"If there is one talent I've developed over the years, Jessica, it's the ability to size up people upon first seeing them. Good hypnotic subjects are generally easygoing, malleable individuals, eager to please others. I observed the audience from backstage and decided on those six. As it turned out, I was right, although two of them were not as easy to work with as the other four. So I concentrated on those four."

Seth smiled, shook his head. "I'd heard that about stage hypnotists," he said, "but you proved it to me tonight. Impressive, Mr. James."

"Thank you, Doctor. Coming from a man of medicine makes it especially complimentary."

"Well," I said, "time for this shopped-out lady—and hypnotic subject—to get to bed. Was I—was I a good subject, Carson? I was once told I wasn't a good hypnotic subject."

"Medium," he replied. "Good enough, as you discovered in your runaway automobile."

I pushed back my chair. "I loved the whole evening, Carson, especially this talk we've had. Makes one think."

"Yes, it does."

Seth paid for the drinks, the bartender called us a cab, we said our goodbyes to Carson, and headed back to the hotel.

"Buy you a drink, or a cup of coffee," I said as we walked into the lobby.

"Had enough to drink," Seth said. "Coffee will keep me awake."

"Decaf won't," I said. "Please. I have a million questions to ask this expert on hypnosis, who I didn't know was an expert.

"I'm no expert."

An hour later, I'd received a primer in hypnosis, including some of Seth's theories about how Sirhan Sirhan might have been programmed to murder Robert Kennedy.

"Whew!" I said as we rode the elevator to Seth's

floor. My room was a few floors above. "Lots to chew on." The doors slid open.

"Don't chew too much, Jessica. Your friend is a nice man. But I still don't think people should use hypnosis in nightclubs."

"Maybe you're right. Sleep tight, Seth. Breakfast at eight?"

"Let's make it seven. Everybody and his brother'll be there by eight."

Chapter Eight

Thanksgiving Day

"What am I most thankful for?"

As a prelude to serving Thanksgiving dinner, I'd asked each of my guests to choose the one thing for which they were most grateful.

Sheriff Morton Metzger chewed his cheek and looked up at the ceiling. "I guess I'm most thankful for all the great friends I have here in Cabot Cove."

His answer brought forth a clapping of hands, and a few "Amens."

Now it was Norman Huffaker's turn. I was pleased to see Norm so relaxed, and enjoying himself. There were no signs of depression in him this night. His hair was neatly combed, and his clothing had that freshly cleaned and pressed look. The French blue knit sweater he wore had the same dramatic effect on his eyes as eyeliner might have. Norm's eyes were shockingly blue. Paul Newman had nothing on him, at least in the eyes department.

"Well, Norm?" I said.

He paused for what seemed an eternity before saying, "I'm thankful, I guess, for the passage of time."

He looked at me and actually blushed. I'd forgotten how shy Norman could be when asked to say something in front of more than a few people, in this case many of them strangers. He didn't strike people as a reticent man, but that was because his outward persona, and reputation as a successful writer, was misleading. One thing I'd noticed over the years was that when he was with his wife, Jill, he was much more outgoing. She gave him a certain confidence, I suppose, that he lacked within himself.

"Passage of time?" Seth Hazlitt said.

"Yes. Because time strengthens friendships." Norm smiled and raised his third glass of white wine. The rest of us returned his toast.

"Thank you, Norm," I said. "That was lovely. And eloquently put."

"No surprise," said Mort Metzger. "After all, he's a writer."

"To the contrary," I said. "Most writers are inarticulate. Including this one."

"Don't be so self-effacing, Jessica," Seth said. "I don't hardly know a more articulate woman."

"Thank you, Seth. But I like to think I write better than I speak. And now, Dr. Hazlitt, speaking of articulate people, it's your turn."

Seth rose. "I have the same thing to say as I did last year, and the year before that, and the year before that. I'm thankful, most of all, for Jessica's hard sauce."

"Hear, hear." There was much laughter.

"What about you, Jess?"

"Hostesses should be seen and not heard," I replied.

"Not on your life. Hostesses should be seen *and* heard."

I peered into my almost empty wineglass, smiled, looked up, and said, "I am very thankful for the beauty that surrounds me every day, and for the good health that allows me to enjoy it. Maine, and this town, is a joy to behold. But even more beautiful is the beauty that emanates from wonderful friendships. I'm one lucky lady to have so much beauty grace my Thanksgiving table. Thank you for sharing this day with me."

"Not bad for an inarticulate woman," said Mort.

Until this moment, most of the conversation had been between myself, and friends of long-standing. But there were others at the table who hadn't as yet been heard. My Thanksgiving guest list had grown considerably since I started putting it together.

Seated next to me was a young man in his early thirties. I'd befriended Jason after having hired him to tend my garden and lawn. Jason didn't have family, at least not to my knowledge, and had been through more foster families in his youth than he could remember. He'd drifted into Cabot Cove a few years ago and stayed, doing odd jobs like gardening, washing dishes, and shoveling snow, with some house painting and car waxing thrown in. He lived alone in a small apartment above Sassi's bakery, where he sometimes helped out in the kitchen.

The assumption of most people in town was that Jason was mildly retarded. But that certainly didn't represent anyone's clinical evaluation. All I knew was that he was a lovely person with a strong work ethic.

So strong, in fact, the minute snow starts to accumulate, Jason's out there shoveling for his regular customers. Ne need to call him, nor does it matter what time the snow arrives. I've awakened more than once in the predawn hours to the steady scrape of his shovel.

"Your turn, dear," I whispered to him.

He mumbled without looking up, "Thank you for inviting me to dinner. It looks delicious. That's all."

I put my arm around him. "I'm so pleased you're here with us, Jason."

Dr. Michael O'Neill, director of the Worrell Institute for Creativity, was next in line to offer special thanks to the gathered. I'd extended the invitation to him and his wife, Amanda, at the last minute, much to the chagrin of Charlene Sassi, whose bakery I'd stormed last night at closing time in search of extra pies. Despite much protestation—"Gory, Jess, this store doesn't have enough room to change your mind"—she found a few extra pies—"For special last-minute people like you"—to round out my dessert menu.

"I'm next?" O'Neill said in mock terror, his hand over his heart.

"You certainly are," I said.

I'd invited the O'Neills yesterday during a phone conversation concerning my upcoming seminars on mystery writing. I casually asked what he was doing for Thanksgiving, and he replied, "No plans."

"Would you join me and my friends?" I asked.

There wasn't any hesitation. "What a lovely gesture," he'd said. "What time would you like Amanda and me to be there?"

O'Neill looked at others around the table and cleared his throat. "I'd like to thank everyone at Cabot Cove for making us—and I speak for myself, my wife, and the Worrell Institute—feel so welcome." He scanned our faces. He and Amanda were certainly welcomed by everyone at my Thanksgiving gathering. But he might have been better served leaving out mention of the Worrell Institute, considering the ominous series of events that had recently occurred there. An uneasy silence spilled over the table.

I sipped my wine. "Amanda?" I said to O'Neill's wife. "I believe you're next."

"Michael said he was speaking for me," she said. Her voice was cold, and distinctly unfriendly.

It had become obvious to me soon after the O'Neills arrived that Amanda did not share her husband's enthusiasm at having accepted my invitation. She'd said little. There are many people whose quiet demeanor at gatherings is appealing, if not welcomed. Amanda O'Neill's taciturn silence, however, spoke of arrogance. But I gave her the benefit of the doubt. Perhaps she was usually gracious and generous in her social skills, but had been angered by something that happened before arriving at my house. I'd met her at the opening gala for the institute; she'd seemed gracious and hospitable enough in that setting.

If my generosity of spirit hadn't been accurately applied, however, I was left with only surprise that she was Dr. Michael O'Neill's wife. He was gregarious and charming. She was—to be kind, a dolt. At least on this day.

Their choice of clothing for a Thanksgiving dinner said much about their differing personalities. Michael wore a navy cashmere blazer, snow-white turtleneck, and gray wool trousers with a razor crease. Amanda, who was tall and slinky, wore a painfully tight black dress cut low in front, massive gold hoop earrings that reached her bare shoulders, and stylish, albeit uncomfortable black platform shoes.

I looked at Michael O'Neill. If his wife's unpleasant refusal to speak had made him uneasy, he wasn't overt in showing it. Trying to put him, as well as everyone else, at ease, I said to Amanda, "That's perfectly all right, Mrs. O'Neill. No need for everyone to have their say."

"I'd like to say something."

The voice belonged to Barbara McCoy, who sat to Amanda's left. She was one of two young women from the Worrell Institute. Once Dr. O'Neill had accepted my invitation—and realizing the dinner table would need an extra leaf or two anyway—I asked whether there were artists at the institute who would be alone on the holiday. He came up with three: Barbara McCoy, a musician; Susan Dalton, the young woman in whom Mort Metzger had taken a liking at the opening party, and who was writing a murder mystery; and a young man, Jo Jo Masarowski, a "video artist" who looked like a poster boy for a FEED THE HUNGRY campaign. There is skinny, and there is pale, but Jo Jo had combined them into an art form of its own.

Barbara McCoy was a striking, although not necessarily attractive woman, who put herself together well, and whose self-confidence made you think of her as beautiful. Model-tall, and pencil-thin, her auburn hair was cropped extremely close, almost a crew cut. Unusually high and defined cheekbones created canyons in which aquamarine eyes dwelled. I pegged her at about the same age Maureen Beaumont had been at the time of her death.

McNeill had told me that Barbara was very much alone in the world. "She doesn't have any family," he'd said. "Her parents were killed in a plane crash two years ago. An only child."

Ms. McCoy spoke slowly, softly, and deliberately. She had stage presence. "I'd like to thank you, Mrs. Fletcher, for inviting me here. May I call you Jessica?"

"Of course."

Amanda O'Neill looked up and squinted at the large brass-and-copper chandelier above the table. Was she asking God for deliverance from the table?

"I'd also like to say something else. I promise I'll make it brief. It's a wonderful tradition you have here, Jessica, having people at your Thanksgiving table express thanks for something special in their lives. Well, along with being thankful for being here with you and your lovely friends, I'm especially grateful for having been accepted to the Worrell Institute. It's been a lifesaver for me. I'm experiencing a major breakthrough. It's incredible. I mean, it's really a special place." She looked at Michael O'Neill with adoring eyes. "I just wish it would stop getting such bad press, so that Dr. O'Neill can get on with the superb work he and his staff are doing."

Amanda's eyes went to her husband—annihilative beams of death and destruction drilling into his brain.

I assumed Barbara was finished, and I was about to ask Susan Dalton if she had anything to add. But then Barbara said, "Maureen Beaumont did not kill herself because of Worrell, even if the institute's critics would like us to think she did. Maureen Beaumont killed herself because she couldn't live with the guilt!"

We all looked at her quizzically. She was aware of the intense interest in her, laughed, and said, "How did I ever get on to *that* subject? Thanks again for inviting me to your table, Jessica."

Amanda O'Neill pushed her chair back so hard it almost fell over, stood, dropped her napkin on it, and left the room. All eyes went to Michael. Certainly, her husband would go after her.

"Time to carve the bird, isn't it?" he said. "May I do the honors?"

"Sorry, Doc, but bird carving is my territory," Mort Metzger said. "Tradition. Every year I get to carve the turkey. Right, Jess?"

Seth said, "Maybe we ought to let a physician do the surgery. Might do a cleaner, better job. Unless, of course, he has other things to tend to." He looked in the direction to which Amanda had made her escape.

"Are you sayin' I don't know how to carve a turkey?" Mort asked.

"No," Seth said. "But we got Dr. O'Neill here. Might be in the holiday spirit to give him a chance."

O'Neill laughed, waved his hands. "I'm a psychiatrist, not a surgeon," he said. "I vote for tradition. The sheriff does the deed."

"Could I—?"

"Yes, Jason?"

"Could I carve the turkey?"

"Well, usually Mort does, and—"

Mort's eyes met mine. He nodded.

"Of course you can, Jason," I said.

"I know how. Miss Sassi taught me."

"Splendid. I'll get you started."

As I led Jason to the kitchen, I glanced at Michael O'Neill, who'd fallen into a spirited conversation with Worrell's resident artists. He seemed jolly enough. But how long would he allow his wife to be absent without checking on her? Maybe she had a set of car keys and had gone home. I silently hoped that was the case. She'd put on a pall on everyone.

I left Jason with the turkey and the necessary tools for carving, and returned to the dining room with a steaming bowl of creamed onions, which I placed in front of O'Neill.

"My favorite," he said.

I decided while in the kitchen that even if Michael wasn't about to check on his wife's whereabouts and well-being, I had an obligation to do so as hostess. I went to the living room where she was huddled in front of the fireplace, her arms wrapped about herself. "Are you all right?" I asked.

"Yes. I mean, I'm not feeling very well."

"I'm sorry. You look cold. Would you like a sweater, a shawl? I have a cashmere one that—"

"I just need some time alone," she said, her eyes fixed on the flickering flames.

"Of course. Come join us when—when you're ready."

Jason had done a masterful job of carving, and was obviously pleased at our acknowledgment of his skill. As we dug in to the bountiful bowls and platters of food, I forgot about Amanda. I think everyone else did, too, including her husband, who ate with gusto. His conversation was as enthusiastic as his appetite.

"More wine?" I asked Norman Huffaker, whose glass was empty. O'Neill's glass had also been drained.

"Sure," Norman said.

As Seth fetched a new bottle of Chablis that was chilling in my refrigerator, I asked Jo Jo Masarowski about video art. That prompted a bits-and-bytes monologue that quickly lost me in its technical jargon. Although I'd recently abandoned my trusty old Remington manual typewriter for a word processor, my knowledge of how it worked was limited to turning it on, and following the simple set of instructions that allowed me to write, store what I'd written on a little disk, and print it out.

Norman had launched into a discussion of wine with Michael O'Neill. They both seemed knowledgeable on the subject. Wine, like computers, was another area of vast mystery to me. I find the ritual of sniffing corks, inhaling fumes, and sipping before sending a bottle back because it "lacks body," or "its bouquet is too timid," to define pretentiousness. It either tastes good or it doesn't.

"Could I have a private word with you?" The question was asked me by Susan Dalton, the blond mystery writer who'd taken up residence at the Worrell Institute.

"Certainly," I said.

We both stood and were about to head for the kitchen when Amanda O'Neill suddenly appeared in the doorway between the dining and living rooms. "Michael," she said sternly.

Michael looked up, returned his attention to the table, and took another hurried fork of chestnut stuffing.

"Michael!" Her voice was louder this time, and more demanding. She disappeared from view.

All attention now focused on him. He sighed, rolled his eyes—the gesture seemed to be directed at Barbara McCoy—stood, stretched, and said, "Excuse me."

"We'll talk in a minute," I said to Susan Dalton.

Although the conversation between the O'Neills was muffled, the tone of their voices clearly indicated that they were having an angry confrontation. Michael returned to the dining room, came to my side, crouched, and whispered in my ear, "I think we'd better be going. Amanda isn't feeling well."

He wished everyone a happy Thanksgiving. I followed him from the room, intending to say goodbye to his wife. But she'd already found her coat and had left the house without a word.

"Thanks for a lovely day, Jessica," O'Neill said. "We must do it again. My house next time."

Unlikely.

I looked through the living room drapes after he left. Amanda was sitting in their car's passenger seat, her arms in a death squeeze around her body, her face a mask of anger. He spun his wheels as he backed from my driveway, and roared up the street.

"What a witch," Barbara McCoy said as I rejoined my guests. Mort and Seth announced they were heading for the den "just to check on bowl game scores." Translation: It was time to watch football. Jason and Jo Jo, who seemed to have taken a liking to each other, went to the kitchen to talk, and to start the cleanup despite my protestations. I was surprised to see that Jason had demonstrated to Jo Jo a knowledge of computers, at least to the extent that he seemed to understand what Jo Jo was talking about. That left me at the table with Susan Dalton, Barbara McCoy, and Norm Huffaker.

Although the two young women seemed friendly enough during dinner, I sensed a certain—call it unease—between them. Nothing overt, just a pulse that I felt, like a low-voltage electrical current.

"It's marvelous that you're enjoying yourself so much at Worrell, and getting so much out of it," I said to Barbara.

"It's a wonderful place," she said eagerly. "Everyone on the staff is outstanding, and I've met so many other interesting artists. It's very inspiring."

"And you, Susan? How is it going for you and the murder mystery you're writing?"

"Better every day."

Barbara announced that she had to return to the institute. "I promised myself I'd have a section of my score completed by morning," she said. "That's one of the things I've learned there. Make a commitment to yourself, and keep it."

"I could use a little of that discipline," I said.

"Maybe you should check in," Norman said, his words slurred from too much wine. His choice of terminology was strange, I thought. "Check in?" Sounded like a hospital, or—mental institution?

"I might just do that," I said.

"Sad, isn't it?" Norm said.

"What's sad?"

"That someone can be so driven by a need to create that she'd kill herself over it."

"Maureen Beaumont," I said.

"Yeah. She became obsessed with her inability to compose something great." He poured himself brandy from a bottle I'd brought to the table. "To feel so blocked, so completely worthless that you blow your brains out. To be that unhappy because you can't create something better than the next guy."

"How about dessert?" I asked, injecting added gaiety into my voice.

Norman went on as though he hadn't heard me. "Why does anybody kill themselves?" he asked no one in particular. "I mean, how is their mind working? What are they thinking? Where's the reasoning?

How is their mind processing what's going on around them?"

"That's what's awesome about the Worrell Institute," said Barbara. "They study just that sort of thing with creative artists."

"Suicide?" I said.

"Yeah," Norm responded. "What makes a blocked artist go over the edge?"

"How do they do that?" I asked.

"In-depth sessions with the artists," Norm said. "The couch. Free association. Behavior mod. Hypnosis."

"Hypnosis," I repeated.

"You were hypnotized last weekend," Norm said, pouring himself another drink he didn't need. I'd told everyone at dinner about my experience in Boston, although I soft-pedaled my brief fling onstage as one of Carson James's hypnotic subjects. "Just playing along," I said, "Show business. It kept the act going." Seth gave me one of his best skeptical looks, but didn't challenge me.

I repeated to Norman that I'd been nothing more than a willing participant in Carson James's show. "Dessert time," I announced. "The pies, and hard sauce, await us."

"I'll go back with you," Norman told Barbara.

"Will you stay awhile?" I asked Susan. "Looks like I'm losing the crowd. I've already lost two of my male friends to 'third-and-long.' "

"Sure," she said.

Jo Jo decided to return to Worrell with Barbara and Norman. I called the cab company that had brought them to the house, and the owner of the service, Jake Monroe, arrived minutes later. He was the only driver that day because none of his employees would work on Thanksgiving. Jake waited inside as his passengers said their goodbyes, and I insisted he take half a pumpkin pie with him. The premature exit by the O'Neills, and now the departure of this contingent, left me with an excess of dessert.

"Last run of the day, Mrs. Fletcher," Jake said. "Wife's got dinner waitin' for me."

"You've certainly earned it," I said.

Susan, Jason, and I cleaned up in the kitchen, then joined Seth and Morton in the den for coffee and pie. The game must not have been too exciting because Seth had dozed off in my recliner, and Mort was reading a newspaper.

"Splendid pie," Seth said after finishing his second piece of apple, with hard sauce, of course.

"Pass your compliments along to Charlene Sassi," I said.

"I have to go home," Jason said.

"I suppose I should, too," said Susan Dalton.

"Oh, I forgot," I said. "You wanted to talk to me about something."

"Yes, I did. Maybe—"

"It also occurs to me," I said, "that you have no way of getting back to the institute. The cab company is closed."

"No problem," Mort said. "Happy to drive Miss Dalton there myself."

"What about Jason?" I asked.

"I'll walk," he said. "I like to walk."

"Drop you off, too," Mort said. "On the way."

"Mind another passenger?" I asked.

"You, Jess?"

"Yes. I could use a ride. Some fresh air."

"Happy to have you," said Mort.

"I'll drive the young lady home," Seth offered

But Mort obviously wanted that pleasure.

We said good night to Seth in front of the house, and I climbed in the backseat of Mort's sheriff's car with Susan Dalton. Jason sat up front.

"What fun," Susan said as Mort started the vehicle and slipped it into gear. "Riding in a sheriff's car."

"Don't say it too loud," I whispered. "I don't think he's supposed to use it for personal reasons."

"I heard ya," Mort said over his shoulder. "The way I figure it, any trip up to Worrell is business. Nasty business."

"I'm going up to the mansion tomorrow," Jason said.

"Are you?" I said. "Why?"

"Jo Jo invited me to see how he makes art on his computer."

"That sounds like fun, Jason. I'm sure you'll enjoy it."

We dropped Jason at Sassi's bakery, and headed up the mountain toward Worrell. I took the opportunity to ask Susan what she'd wanted to speak with me about.

"I can tune out if you want it to be private," Mort said.

"Oh, no," Susan said. "What I have to say would be of interest to Sheriff Metzger."

"Well, then, we're all ears," I said.

"It's about Maureen Beaumont and how she died."

"Yes?"

"And the other girl who tried to commit suicide."

"Hear from Seth she's gonna be okay," Mort said.

"That's good," said Susan. "I think she really did try to kill herself."

"Why would you even doubt it?" I asked.

"Because people say that Maureen Beaumont killed herself."

We waited.

"She didn't."

"She didn't?" Mort and I said in unison.

"She was murdered. And I think I know who did it."

If we were "all ears" before, our auditory receptivity was now at its peak setting.

"Maureen was a jealous person," Susan continued. "Very jealous. And competitive. She was depressed because she wasn't doing as well as some of the other musicians. Including Barbara."

"Ms. McCoy? Who was at my house today?"

"Yes. When Barbara found out that Maureen had stolen her score, and was using it for her own project, she was furious. She was so mad, she—she was ready to kill."

Mort pulled off the winding road and parked on the shoulder. He turned and said, "Are you sayin', Ms. Dalton, that Miss McCoy shot Maureen Beaumont?"

"I'm saying—yes, I think she did."

"*Think?*" Mort said.

"Yes. Unbelievable, isn't it?"

"Well, yes, I'd certainly agree with that assessment. But you have to be more certain, Susan. It's a very serious charge you're making."

"I'm aware of that." My mild rebuke caused her to pout.

"Got any proof?" Mort asked.

"No. But I'm working on it."

"How are you doing that?" I asked.

"Listening. Observing. You know, Jessica, when I first met you at the party, I didn't know who you were. I've never read much. Not since school. But when I found out how famous you are as a mystery writer, it sort of—well, it inspired me. You can imagine how tickled I was to be invited to your house for Thanksgiving dinner."

"The pleasure was mine, Susan."

"I never was sold on that suicide theory regardin' Miss Beaumont," Mort said.

"I remember you expressing that," I said. "The powder burns, wasn't it?"

"Yup."

"See?" Susan said with animation. "Of course. The powder burns."

"You know about powder burns?" I asked.

"I know that if you hold a gun to your head, it leaves powder burns. There weren't any. That's it!"

"Susan," I said, "there were powder burns, weren't there, Mort?"

"Yup, except that—"

I interrupted. "Susan, this kind of speculation is interesting, of course. But you have to be careful about expressing your theories until you've gathered enough facts. Evidence."

"And that's exactly what I intend to do, Jessica. Imagine. A murder takes place before my very eyes. I was absolutely at a loss for a plot for my book. I didn't have one idea that made sense. I talked about it during my therapy sessions with Dr. O'Neill and his staff. They're so terrific, so supportive. They're working on getting me to open my mind so that the creative juices can flow freely."

"I see."

"So I've been trying to do that. And then it hit me. The story is right in front of my eyes. It's for real. All I have to do is follow it, and turn it into a plot based on real life."

"Uh-huh."

Mort started to pull back onto the road, but I stopped him. "Tell me more about this stolen music," I said to Susan.

"It's not difficult to prove, Jessica. I heard Maureen playing it the night before she died. I thought it sounded so pretty, so I went into the practice room to tell her. She panicked, covered the music with other papers. That seemed strange to me, but I didn't say anything.

"Then, later that night, I heard an argument in the practice room. I kind of pressed my ear to the door. Barbara McCoy was in there with Maureen. She was yelling at her about how Maureen stole her musical score. Maureen denied it, but they kept yelling at each other. Finally, I heard Barbara say something like if Maureen tried to claim the score as her own, she'd kill her."

"She said that?" Mort said. "In exactly those words?"

"Something like that."

Mort and I exchanged glances.

"Is that what Barbara meant when she said Maureen Beaumont had killed herself because she 'couldn't live with the guilt?'" I asked.

"I bet that's what she meant," Susan replied.

"Well, Susan," I said, "this has been—fascinating."

"I thought you'd think it was," she said. "Can I count on you and Sheriff Metzger to help me?"

"Help you?"

"Solve the murder. That would be good for you, Sheriff. And I'd have a plot for my book,"

"I think we'd better get going, Mort," I said.

We were stopped at the gate by an institute security guard, who allowed us to pass once he saw it was Mort, and that one of the institute's residents was being returned to the mansion.

"Good night, Susan," I said.

"Good night, Jessica. Thank you again for having me to dinner. It was yummy."

"You take care," Mort said. "Leave the solvin' of murders to me."

"Oh, I will. I'll call you when I find out more." She was out of the car, bounded up the steps, and disappeared inside.

"What do you think?" I asked Mort.

"She's a pretty thing," he replied.

"I don't mean her looks. I mean her theory."

He shrugged. "Wish she wouldn't go snoopin' around like that," he said. "If that Beaumont woman was murdered, isn't likely the murderer will appreciate havin' her stickin' her nose into it."

"My thought exactly."

Chapter Nine

Once upon a time, I lived in large cities, and loved them. Their energy matched perfectly with my youthful sense of purpose and exploration.

But now that I've lived in the small town of Cabot Cove, Maine, all these years, I can't imagine ever living in a metropolis again. The inherent peace and beauty it offers has captured me for life. It is a place to which I yearn to return whenever I travel.

My house is not large, nor is it lavishly decorated and furnished. It fits me like a well-worn slipper, and if I were to win the state lottery—which I play religiously, one ticket a week—there's nothing I would change with my house, or my life.

But that's not to say that Cabot Cove doesn't have its drawbacks. Like any small town, it lacks certain amenities, particularly in the area of culture. The hope that by attracting young artists and musicians to the town, the Worrell Institute for Creativity would foster a cultural center, had not happened. At least not yet.

Another characteristic of small towns is the penchant for gossip. Everyone knows everyone else—or at least it seems that way—which means it isn't easy to get lost. And we all need to lose ourselves on occasion, if only for a day or two. The problem is that, by some strange process, what you've done while hibernating is quickly known around town. Rent a batch of videos for a weekend and someone on Monday will ask how you enjoyed the films, by name. Subscribe to a controversial publication and it will be known. There's nothing malicious about it. It just happens.

When I wrote my first novel in my new Cabot Cove house, speculation ran rampant in town. I was antisocial. I was hiding a demented family member in the attic. Those rumors eventually abated, but the absurdity of some of them lingers with me to this day.

Now, a few days after Thanksgiving, I was to hear another rumor about me. You'd think that having lived for so many years in a small town environment, I wouldn't be shocked at what Sheriff Morton Metzger told me when he stopped by at my house for coffee.

"You've got to be kidding! That's ridiculous! Insane! Crazy!"

He'd given me the news between bites of English muffin, tossed it at me as though he was announcing a forecast of snow, or that his budget for a new patrol car had been approved.

"Calm down, Jess. Just a damn rumor circulatin' about town this mornin'."

"But it doesn't make any sense. Why on earth

would anyone suspect me? What possible motive would I have for wanting Maureen Beaumont dead?"

"Seems I might be at the root of it."

"You? How?"

"Not so much that you would be a suspect, but that the rumor ever got started in the first place. I never closed the book on Miss Beaumont's death. Never bought suicide. You know that as well as I do."

"Yes, I do."

"That's the problem, Jess. Folks got the drift that I was continuin' to investigate, so they put two and two together, and they figure that if I think the woman was murdered, that means there's got to be a murderer."

"Your reasoning is impressive. Go on."

"So, everybody's got a theory. You know how folks can be."

"I understand all that, Mort. But why *me*?"

He laughed.

"It's not funny, Mort."

"Better to have a sense of humor about such things, Jess."

"Who said it?" I asked. "Who mentioned me as a possible suspect?"

"That doesn't matter much." He finished his muffin.

"It matters to me."

"I don't think Sybil meant anything by it. Sort of a joke."

"Sybil?"

"Ayuh."

"Sybil Stewart? Our mayor?"

"Down at Mara's this mornin'. Just gossipin' with a bunch a' other ladies."

"Sybil Stewart brought up my name as a suspect?"

"You know Sybil, Jess. Got herself a big mouth, like all politicians."

"Bigger than most."

I'd been named a suspect in a few cases before. In those instances, I could usually make sense of it. I'd ended up in the wrong place at the wrong time, or with the wrong people.

But I couldn't for the life of me understand why Sybil Stewart would have mentioned my name in connection with Maureen Beaumont's death. Obviously, she didn't buy the suicide story any more than Morton did. Of course, the fact that he continued to investigate—and undoubtedly talked too much about it over coffee at Mara's—contributed to everyone's skepticism.

Mort wiped his mouth with his napkin and stood. "Got to be goin', Jess. Coffee and muffin hit the spot." He shook his head and laughed.

"I'm sorry, Mort, but I don't find this at all funny."

"Oh, you know Sybil, Jess. Suspicious of everything. She didn't mean nothin' by it."

If I didn't know better, I'd think he was defending Sybil Stewart because, as mayor, she was his boss. Of course, he didn't have to tell me about Sybil's stupid comment at Mara's. But he knew I'd find out eventually through the active Cabot Cove grapevine. Better to have come from him, was the way he'd probably processed it.

"Well, Mort, I repeat that I'm incapable of sharing

this laugh with you. I find what Sybil has said to be slanderous."

The moment Mort left, the phone rang. I hastily wiped my fingers clean of the boysenberry jam I'd been enjoying on a pecan scone—I abhor sticky telephones—and answered.

"Jessica. Michael O'Neill here. Sounds like you've been sitting by the phone waiting for my call." It had been a week since he and his wife were my guests for Thanksgiving.

"Maybe I was," I said. "How are you, Michael?"

"Fine. Just fine. I call for two reasons, Jessica. First, to thank you for a lovely Thanksgiving dinner. I was honored to be at your table. Second—and this is more difficult—I must apologize, once again, for our sudden departure. Amanda's feeling much better now. It came over her so quickly at your house. A wicked, sudden virus. She's just now feeling like her old self. So much flu around these days."

No one I knew had the flu, I thought. And what was Amanda O'Neill's "old self?"

"I'm glad to hear that," I said. "That Amanda is feeling better. Sorry that you couldn't stay for dessert. They say my hard sauce this year was exceptionally good."

"And I'm looking for a rain check, Jessica. I've been thinking about what I missed ever since."

There was an awkward pause.

"Jessica, there's another reason I've called. Perhaps more serious."

"Yes?"

"I'm calling regarding your friend, Norman Huffaker."

"What about him?"

"You've known him for quite some time. Correct?"

"Yes. A very long time."

His silence said that he wanted *me* to say something about Norman. But I wasn't about to offer information concerning my friend. I broke the silence. "Is this about Norm's work? I haven't seen him since Thanksgiving. I assume he's progressing nicely, is conquering his writer's block."

"I really don't know, Jessica. That's why I'm calling. Do you know where he is?"

"Know where he is? Is he missing?"

O'Neill's laugh was designed to dismiss such a thought. He said, "We haven't seen him for a couple of days now. Last time anyone saw him was Monday afternoon. I thought he might have decided to stay with a friend. Like you."

"Monday? That's three days ago, Michael. No, he hasn't come here. You sound concerned."

"Not at all. But I did feel it warranted calling you."

"Maybe he went back home to California," I offered. "Are his belongings still there?"

"Yes. That's the odd thing. His clothes are still in his room. He even left his computer on. Next to it was a snifter that still had brandy in it."

"Well," I said lightly, "I'm sure he'll turn up. I can recall a few times when Norman picked up and disappeared, much to his wife's chagrin." I didn't add that such absences never lasted more than twenty-four hours, or that he always called Jill to keep her from worrying. "If I hear from him, I'll give you a call."

"Thank you, Jessica. And again, thank you for a lovely day."

I hung up, opened my address book to "H" and dialed Jill Huffaker's number in Los Angeles. She answered in her familiar singsong voice.

"Hello, Jill. It's Jess."

"Great minds think alike. I was just about to pick up the phone and call you."

"Oh?"

"I spoke to Norm a couple of days ago. Monday, I guess it was. He sounded okay, although he said the script wasn't coming along that good. I thought I'd get a report on my blocked husband from you."

He wasn't in California.

I'd hoped that Jill would have said Norm had impetuously decided to come home, that he was over his writer's block, and didn't need to be at Worrell any longer. I wanted to hear that. But didn't.

"Jess?"

"What? Oh, sorry, Jill. I was distracted by something."

"How is Norm? He said he had a wonderful time at your house on Thanksgiving."

"Yes. We had a lovely day."

"Is Norm—?"

"Norm is—Norm is fine, last I heard."

My hand inadvertently moved, knocking the plate with my half-eaten scone to the floor.

"Drop something, Jess?"

"Yes. Clumsy me. Can I get back to you? I'd better

clean up this mess before my bleached white wood floor looks like a Jackson Pollock painting."

She laughed. "Sure. No rush. Say hello to my dear hubby for me."

"I will."

I hung up with a sigh of relief—as well as a dose of guilt for not having been forthright with my friend—and pressed an auto-dial number on my phone. Mort Metzger answered promptly. "Mort, it's Jess. I need to talk to you."

"I'm listening, Jessica."

"Can I come to the office?"

"Now?"

"Yes. Right now. I think I might have to file a missing-person's report."

Chapter Ten

"Seems to me you might be jumpin' the gun, Jess."

I sat across the desk from Mort Metzger and felt my frustration level rise.

"Maybe you should talk to some more people," he said. "You know, other friends of his. He might just have picked up and gone away for a couple of days with one of them."

"That's always a possibility," I said. "But I don't consider it a probability."

Mort's tiny, snide laugh was annoying. "You know how writers are, Jess. Not the most stable of people."

"Pardon?"

"Present company excepted. Is Norman Huffaker the sort of person who'd take up with a woman on a whim?"

"I don't think so. I spoke with his wife in California. They have a good relationship. I think."

He rolled his eyes up to the ceiling.

"I have to admit, Morton, that your lack of a sense of urgency in this matter is disconcerting."

"All I'm saying, Jessica, is that maybe he needed to get away from it all for a couple of days." He'd obviously sensed my frustration with him and was attempting to soften his bedside manner. "I suggest we take it slow. Chances are your friend is just fine. But I'll get one of the boys to make some calls. Local bed-and-breakfasts. Hotels."

I stood firm. "Look, Mort," I said. "Norman Huffaker is missing. No one has seen him since Monday. He's not the type to simply disappear, at least not for this number of days. He would have called Jill, his wife. Or me. We're wasting precious time."

Mort leaned back, folded his hands across his chest, and fixed me over half-glasses. "You tell his wife her husband's missing?"

"No."

"Why not?"

"Because I didn't want to unduly worry her. I thought—maybe he isn't 'missing.' Maybe he's just gone away for a few days."

Mort's expression said, That's what I just said.

"But I changed my mind the minute I got off the phone with her. I'm worried, Mort. Michael O'Neill said Norman left all his clothing behind. And his computer was on."

The sheriff shrugged.

"I want to file an official missing-person's report."

"Don't you think that's up to Huffaker's wife to do? Her call?"

"I suppose so." I took a deep breath. "Let me call her back, tell her what's happened here, and get her permission to file a report. May I use your phone?"

He gestured to the phone on his desk. I dialed

Jill's number. "Hello?" Jill answered on the first ring. Her voice wasn't singsong this time. It was a panicked "hello."

"Jill. It's Jess."

"Jessica. Thank God it's you. I don't know what to do. Norman phoned me right after our conversation." She started to cry.

"Jill. What's wrong?"

"You won't believe this, Jess. I sure don't. He said—he said he was going to kill himself." She got it out through what had become uncontrollable sobs.

"Did he say where he was?"

"No. I'm sorry. I didn't mean to fall apart like this."

"That's all right. You have no idea where he was calling from?"

"No. I assumed he was calling from the Worrell Institute. I called them, but they said he wasn't there. It was so strange, Jess."

"What was strange?"

"It didn't—sound like Norman. He was either very drunk, or disguising his voice. Why would he want to do that?"

"I can't imagine. Are you saying you aren't sure it was him?"

"It was him. I mean, I think it was. He said it was him. His voice sounded—well, like his—but then it didn't. It was such a short conversation. Less than a minute. He mumbled that he couldn't take it any more, and that I'd be better off without him. I tried to ask where he was, but he just rambled on, almost like it was a script. He ended by saying he'd always love me. He hung up. The phone went dead. I screamed his name, but there was only a dial tone."

"It must have been him, Jill. Why would anyone else call and say such a dreadful thing?"

"I don't know. I need your help, Jess. What should I do?" She'd started sobbing again. "I feel so helpless. I'm so far away. I thought of getting on the next flight, but I don't want to leave in case he calls again. I'm even afraid to be talking to you and tying up the line. I've got to talk to him. I had no idea he was this distraught."

"Jill, just sit tight. I agree you shouldn't leave in case he tries to contact you again. Chances are he will. I'll call you at regular intervals. In the meantime, I'll do whatever I can to find him on this end."

"Thanks, Jess. You are a friend."

It occurred to me when I hung up that I hadn't told Jill about Michael O'Neill's call that alerted me to Norm's disappearance in the first place. Nor had I mentioned I was sitting in Sheriff Metzger's office about to file a missing-person's report. She would assume I was home, and might try me there. I considered calling her back right away, but decided against it. I wanted to expedite things with Mort.

I called my machine to see if I'd received any calls, hopefully one from Norm. No such luck.

Mort had left me alone in the room while I spoke with Jill. I looked through an interior window that separated his office from the main one. He was on the telephone. Judging from his expression and gestures, it was not a pleasant conversation. He slammed the receiver down into the cradle, spun around in the swivel chair, and looked at me through the glass.

I motioned for him to return. I wanted to fill him in on what I'd learned from Jill Huffaker.

"Mort," I said as he closed the door behind him, "I really am upset at your intractability. I've just learned that—"

"I know," he said, sitting heavily in his chair. "I'm sorry."

His sudden change of tune, and apology, threw me off guard. Usually, the expression on Mort's face was animated. But all animation was now gone. His face was one of those Magna Doodle screens on which I could have written anything.

"I'm really sorry, Jess," he repeated.

"It's okay. I just spoke to Norm's wife, Jill, and I want to get the report filed and—Mort. What's wrong?"

"Bad news, Jess," he said. "Bobby just called in. He's on patrol down to the Old Moose River Bridge. He came across a red BMW parked there. Engine running. Bob checked the plate with Central. Car belongs to a doctor up at the Worrell Institute. A Dr. Tomar Meti. Met him at the party when they opened the place."

"Yes. I know him."

"Meti filled a stolen car report this mornin'."

"And?"

"And—Damn, Jess, I hate to break this news to you, but looks like I don't have any choice. Bobby says there was a suicide note in the car."

"Oh, my God," I muttered.

"They're puttin' together a search team now. With this damn nor'easter bearin' down on us today, the river is real choppy. Got a nasty blizzard due in overnight."

"Did Bobby tell you if the note was signed?"

He nodded.

"Norman Huffaker?"

"Afraid so, Jess."

Chapter Eleven

The writer's only responsibility is to his art. He must be ruthless if he is to be a good one. He has a dream. It anguishes him so terribly that he must rid himself of it. He has no peace until then. Everything must take second place to his art—honor, pride, decency, security, happiness—all to break through and to write. If a writer has to rob his mother in order to fulfill his dream, he will not hesitate.

My dear Jill, to paraphrase Faulkner, I am guilty of robbery. And I have failed. My dream is gone. I will always love you. Norman.

The snowstorm that was supposed to begin overnight snuck in earlier than the weather pundits had forecast. The ground was already covered when I returned home from Mort Metzger's office and called Jill. She was considerably calmer now, although the strain in her voice came through.

Had I felt I had a choice, I would not have elected to be the one to break the news to her about the abandoned car, and Norm's suicide note. But I didn't see any alternative. I could have prevailed upon Mort to make the call as Cabot Cove's chief law enforcement officer. But not only was that unfair, it would have represented cowardice on my part. Norman and Jill Huffaker were friends. As traumatic as the news would be to Jill, having it come from a friend would hopefully soften the blow, if only a little.

Jill listened patiently as I recounted the events: Michael O'Neill's call informing me of Norman's disappearance; my meeting with Mort Metzger, during which I asked that a missing-person's report be filed; Mort's call from his deputy about having found the car belonging to Dr. Tomar Meti, and Meti's stolen vehicle report; and, of course, the note.

"Sheriff Metzger has the original," I told her. "One of his deputies brought it to headquarters just as I was leaving there. Mort let me make a photocopy in his office. I can read it to you."

"No, Jess. Please don't."

"Sure?"

"Yes. I don't know—having someone else, even a dear friend like you, read it seems—well, wrong. Do you understand?"

"Of course I do."

"I'll be coming to Cabot Cove. I'll read it then."

"All right."

She sighed deeply. It sounded as though she was in the room with me. "It was the drinking," she said absently.

I said nothing.

"Drinking is a depressant, you know. In retrospect, Norm needed to be at Betty Ford's addiction facility, not at this Worrell Institute for Creativity. He didn't need help being creative. He was the most creative person I've ever known. His writer's block wasn't because his creative juices had dried up. It was because he'd been drinking so heavily. You know how Norm always tended to be depressed, without the help of alcohol. Some drunks get rowdy, some get happy. Norm just got more depressed. I wish I'd had the wisdom to have seen it for what it really was. Maybe I could have—"

"Don't blame yourself, Jill."

"I'm not assigning blame, Jess. I know that's a futile exercise. Not rational. Still—"

"I'm going out to where they found the car next to the Moose River," I said. "Sheriff Metzger doesn't want me to, but I'd feel better seeing with my own eyes what the situation is."

"Jess."

"Yes?"

"Do you think that maybe Norm is—alive?"

"I think that's a very good possibility," I said. I lightened my voice. "He is, after all, an imaginative writer. Maybe he needed to do this for—well, for a plot or something." I knew my statement was illogical, even absurd. But I needed to say something comforting.

It seemed to work, at least for that moment. Jill brightened. "That's what I think," she said.

"I'll be back in about an hour," I said. "I'd better get going. We have a blizzard rolling in ahead of schedule. It's coming down pretty hard right now."

"Careful driving," Jill said. "I remember those

Maine blizzards. That's why we moved to sunny California."

I forced a laugh. "You know I don't drive. Our trusty local cab company will do the honors. Stay right there in sunny California, Jill. I'll get back to you in an hour or so. Somehow, I have this crazy notion that your phone is going to ring, you'll pick up, and it will be Norman."

"I pray you're right, Jess."

Before my cab arrived, I placed a call to Michael O'Neill's home. Amanda answered.

"Hello, Amanda. This is Jessica Fletcher."

"Hello." Her tone was as cold as the icicles hanging outside my kitchen window.

"I understand you're feeling better," I said.

"Much."

So much for small talk. "Amanda, is Michael there?"

"He's in the shower."

"Oh. Would you be good enough to give him a message?" I took her silence as an affirmation that she would. "I'd like to swing by Worrell today and pick up Norman Huffaker's personal things. I understand they've been gathered. I'll ask the police to authorize their release to me."

"I'll tell Michael."

"Thank you. Have a pleasant day."

Jake Monroe pulled up a few minutes later in his taxi. He wore a Russian fur hat, and three layers of plaid flannel shirts. Jake didn't wear a beard, but always looked like he was about to sprout one. I got in the front seat. "Moose River," I said.

"Down to the bridge where they found the car?"

"Yes. I suppose it's all over town by now."

He laughed. "Have a couple of hundred gawkers there by now if it was summertime. Snow'll keep 'em away."

"How are the roads?" I asked as he pulled away.

"Mite greezy, Mrs. Fletcher. But I got my chains on. No problem."

Jake had the taxi's radio tuned to a local station. A newscaster, whose voice testified to his youth, gave the headlines, ending with: "Noted writer is an apparent Cabot Cove suicide. Stay tuned for details."

After a slew of commercials, the newscaster returned:

"*A well-known screenwriter, here from California to attend the Worrell Institute for Creativity, is believed to have taken his own life early this morning by jumping off the Old Moose River Bridge. A note was found in a car parked on the bridge with its engine running. The car was reported stolen by one of the institute's physicians, Dr. Tomar Meti. The writer, Norman Huffaker, is alleged to have left the suicide note, according to Cabot Cove sheriff, Morton Metzger. No body has been recovered, and the search is being hampered by the storm. Huffaker is a close friend of noted Cabot Cove mystery writer, Jessica Fletcher. Now for more on what Ol' Man Winter's got in store for us, here's Lou Furino . . .*"

I looked out the vehicle's window into a swirling mass of white. Jake navigated a curve, and the taxi slid in the direction of a snowbank from a previous storm. "Not to worry," he said, turning in the direction of the skid and bringing the car under control.

The announcer's weather forecast was grim. I suppose circumstances made it seem more ominous than it ordinarily might have been for me. I'm a self-confessed weather junkie. I set out in college to become a meteorologist, but vetoed that career when I took a first glance at the four-year curriculum. Too much math for this undergrad. I became an instant English major.

I wondered how my name had been linked to Norm's. Not that our relationship was a secret. But the local station had obviously been informed of the friendship. I assumed Mort had been the source, although it was hardly the sort of information a sheriff would consider important when talking to the press.

By the time we reached the Old Moose River Bridge, which spanned the Moose River at one of its narrower points, visibility had been reduced to the length of your arm. The Moose River is a favorite of white-water rafters in the summer months. I don't speak from experience. Walking and bicycle riding are more my cup of tea, although I do enjoy a dip in the ocean in late August when the sun's been around long enough to have effectively heated the frigid Atlantic.

Jake pulled up behind Mort Metzger's car, whose flashing red roof lights, turning in concert with the lights of other police vehicles, created an eerie, colorful show as their beams were caught by the blowing snow.

I pulled the collar of my coat up tight about my

throat, tightened my scarf across my mouth and nose, and walked to where Mort and some of his officers were attempting to mount a search for Norm's body.

"Shouldn't be here, Jess," Mort said, his white breath mingling with the white snow.

"Couldn't stay away," I said. "Any luck?"

"Nope. Got to call it off right now."

I saw a maroon BMW parked on the bridge. "Is that Dr. Meti's car?" I asked.

"Ayuh."

"Find anything in it?" I asked.

"The note. You saw it."

"Anything else?"

"Haven't had a good look yet. Do that once we get it back to the vehicle pound."

He barked an order that everyone was to pack up and return to headquarters. "Bobby, drive the BMW back."

"Yes, sir."

Mort walked me to Jake's taxi.

"Something's not right here," I said.

"What's not right, Jessica, is the weather. No sense froggin' around any longer. Suggest you get on home and ride this out in front of your fireplace."

"Probably won't have a choice," I said. "Mort, is it all right for me to go to Worrell and pick up Norman's personal belongings? I know his wife would want that."

"Don't see why not. I'd like to take a look at 'em, but won't get there today. Suppose I'd feel better knowin' they were in your possession."

"I'll keep everything safe. Will you call Worrell and tell them it's okay for me to get them?"

"Ayuh."

"And you'll keep me posted?"

"You know I will." To Jake: "You drive easy now. Get her home in one piece."

Jake scowled at Mort, put the taxi in reverse, managed to turn around on the narrow, icy road, and delivered me to my front door.

"Thanks, Jake," I said. There was no need to pay him. Because I don't drive, I use Jake on a regular basis, and have a house account.

I was about to pour myself a cup of divine vanilla almond coffee, a pound of which Seth Hazlitt had given me, when the phone rang.

"Hello?"

"Jessica. Michael O'Neill here."

"Yes, Michael?"

"How are you holding up?"

"All right. I haven't had time to fall apart."

"Any word on whether they've found the body?"

"Nothing yet. I just came from the river. They had to abandon the search because of the weather. Sheriff Metzger will keep me updated."

"I was thinking I should call Mrs. Huffaker. Do you agree?"

"I think it might be premature, Michael. I'll be talking with Jill in a few minutes. I'll tell her of your concern. If she wishes to talk with you, I'm sure she'll call. I convinced her to stay in California until there's something more definitive about Norman. No chance of her coming here anyway. Not with this weather. I just heard on CNN that the storm could be one of the worst in decades. Shutting everything down from Georgia to Canada."

"How is Mrs. Huffaker doing?" he asked.

"As good as can be expected. Not knowing for certain makes it harder, I suppose."

"There's no doubt, is there, that he's—I mean, that Mr. Huffaker took his life?"

"*I* have serious doubts," I said.

"I see. Hopefully, you'll be proved right."

"I'm still hoping to swing by and pick up Norm's things," I said. "Depends on the weather."

"Pick up his things?"

"Yes. Didn't Amanda give you my message? You were in the shower."

"No, she didn't. Oh. That's what this note is about."

"What note?"

"Ms. Portledge left me a note. Sheriff Metzger called to say Mr. Huffaker's possessions could be released to you. I wasn't sure what it meant."

"I assume there's no problem," I said.

"No. No problem. I just wasn't prepared for it. Let's see. I've got his computer in my office. I'm tied up in meetings all day. Another blot on Worrell. I spend more time on damage control than on the mission of this institution."

I was about to say "I'm sorry," but decided not to bother. Undoubtedly, the trio of "suicides," one successful, one leaving the individual in a hospital, and now a missing body, was bad for business at Worrell. But I resented having Norman considered a "blot."

"I'll arrange to leave the computer at the reception desk."

"There are other things as well, Michael. Norman's personal belongings. Are they still in his room?"

"Yes. It's been sealed off. I'll have everything at Reception."

"Fine. It just occurred to me, Michael, that Amanda isn't the only forgetful person this morning. You and I were to meet concerning the seminars."

"We were?"

"I think so. Just as well we push it off to another day."

"I agree. Time to get to my first meeting. Thank you for calling."

I'd no sooner hung up on O'Neill when the phone rang again.

"Hello?"

Dead air.

"Hello? Hello? Anybody there?"

A wrong number? Or Norm? Why did I even think that was a possibility? Denial, I suppose. Until they dragged his body from the river, I preferred to think he was still alive.

I finished what was left of my lukewarm coffee, and called Jake's Cab Company. "Jake, it's Jessica. I need to go to the Worrell Institute."

He grunted. "Looked out your window lately?" he said.

"Yes. It's a blizzard."

"Good day to stay home, Mrs. Fletcher."

"I know that, Jake. I suppose what I have to do at

Worrell could wait a day or two. But I want to do it today. Don't think we'd make it?"

"Make it? Of course we can make it."

I smiled. My challenge was working.

"Might be a slow ride."

"Slow and safe. That's your motto, isn't it?"

"All right. Be there soon as I can."

"And don't forget your chains."

I put on a heavy purple, angora wool pullover sweater—my special "blizzard sweater"—boots, scarf, mittens, and hat, and waited for Jake to arrive.

Chains or no chains, we did a lot of slipping and sliding as Jake navigated the narrow, ascending road leading to the Worrell Mansion. "Maybe this wasn't such a great idea," I said.

"I can handle it," he said, his eyes fixed on what could be seen of the road in front of us. "Got thirty-five-years experience driving in this neck of the woods, Mrs. Fletcher. Not even a fender bender. Out-of-towners cause all the problems. Don't know what in hell they're doin' in snow."

"I've noticed," I said. I thought back to having been in New York City the previous winter. It snowed less than two inches one day, but the entire city was paralyzed. They say New Yorkers are tough, can handle muggings, pollution, roaches, and grid-lock. But when it comes to snow, even umbrellas go up. Washington, D.C. is even worse. The first sign of ice and the city shuts down. If I were a nation planning an attack on the United States, it would be launched during an ice storm in the nation's capital. No one in government comes to work.

"Like him," Jake said as a car approached from the opposite direction. After we'd safely passed each other, Jake muttered, "Probably break his damn fool neck by the time he gets down to the bottom."

"Jake, do you ever think about leaving Cabot Cove and moving to somewhere where it's warm in winter? Florida? California?"

"Nope. Like it just fine right here."

"I have a friend who went to California from here because he hated cold and snow."

"That so?"

"Yes. Norman Huffaker. The man they say killed himself this morning at Moose River."

"Uh-huh."

"He hated snow. Especially driving in it. This may sound silly, but I don't think he would have picked the day of a blizzard to kill himself, to drive on these roads."

Jake laughed. "Seems to me when a fella decides to kill himself, he ain't goin' to worry about gettin' into an automobile accident."

"I suppose you're right. Still, knowing Norm."

Norm despised snow. "Just think, I'll never have to drive in this stuff again," he'd joked at his going-away party. "It's not civilized to have to contend with ice and snow just to run out for a quart of milk." His gloating over escaping to a warmer climate evidently made someone up there angry, because it snowed an unprecedented thirty-seven inches the next day, delaying Norm and Jill's flight to California by two days. "Must have been a jealous God who got himself demoted to the Northeast," he'd said.

Michael O'Neill was standing at the reception desk when I entered the lobby. I'd invited Jake in, but he declined. "Place gives me the creeps," he'd said, opting to wait in his cab.

"Hello there, Jessica. I'm surprised to see you here. The weather is dreadful."

"I really wanted to get Norm's things, Michael. I have a taxi waiting outside. Is everything ready to go?"

"Yes. All here, as promised."

I surveyed the items in front of me. A Compac laptop computer in a padded case, a suitcase, two smaller bags, and a box labeled, MISCELLANEOUS. I couldn't help but smile. The computer case, smaller boxes, and even the suitcase were labeled. Jill Huffaker had bought her husband one of those Brother label makers a few birthdays ago, and he never went anywhere without it. He loved that label maker. According to Jill, he labeled everything, tapes, dresser drawers, tools, even wrapped Christmas presents.

"I assume everything is here," I said.

"I'm sure it is."

"His computer disks? Are they in with the computer?"

"His disks? I'm sure they are."

Jake saw me open the door, and came up the stairs to help. We put everything in the trunk except for the computer.

"Thanks, Michael," I said. "Get inside before you turn into a snowman."

"Where to, Mrs. Fletcher?" Jake asked as he pulled away.

"Home, I guess. And I promise this is the last call from me today."

Chapter Twelve

A Few Days Later

The blizzard that had paralyzed the entire East Coast eventually blew out to sea, as blizzards usually do, leaving behind a lovely white blanket to hide the inconvenience, and occasional misery.

I didn't leave my house once I'd returned home from Worrell with Norm's personal effects. Even if I'd wanted to venture out, I doubted whether Jake would have been able, or willing to take me despite his treasured chains.

Jason showed up the minute the snowfall showed signs of abating. I watched from the window as he attacked the massive snowdrifts with a determined, steady rhythm. It took the better part of the day for him to dig me out sufficiently so that I could reach the mailbox, garbage cans, cottage at the rear of my property, and other mundane destinations that we take for granted—until we can't get to them.

I didn't mind the forced isolation. It wouldn't have mattered if I had. Mother Nature was firmly in control. When that happens, the best we can do is duck as many punches as possible, and conserve energy for when "she" tires.

Because I was housebound during the storm, I got a lot of work done. I'd stopped work on *Brandy & Bullets*—too many distractions. But I did have a seminar to teach at Worrell in a few days.

Considering the weather, to say nothing of Norm Huffaker's disappearance, I considered canceling it. Norm's body still hadn't been found. The clearing weather meant that Mort Metzger's department, in concert with a state team of officers, could resume their search. But no one seemed optimistic that their efforts would be fruitful. The Moose River, relatively free-flowing when the storm hit, was now frozen over. No telling where the body—if there was a body—might have ended up. Probably frozen beneath the river's surface. If that was the case, only the spring thaw would reveal its whereabouts.

I kept in close touch with Jill. She seemed to be accepting the situation with admirable aplomb. As much as I wanted to deliver promising news to her, I was careful not to plant false and misleading hopes. All I could do was assure her that I would keep tabs on progress in Cabot Cove, and report to her as things developed.

She seemed less anxious to travel to Cabot Cove than before. I told her I'd picked up Norm's things, which seemed to make her feel better. "No sense in coming here, Jill, until—*unless* they find Norm. You're better off staying where you are."

My flirtation with canceling the seminar had to do

with more than Norman Huffaker, and the weather. Truth is, I was nervous about doing it. I don't consider myself a teacher, although I have found myself in front of a class on a few occasions, the most recent in New York City where I lectured on criminal detection.

But I wasn't any more comfortable with that situation than I was with the contemplation of standing before a group of artists, writers, and musicians at Worrell, and telling them how to write a murder mystery. The reality is that I don't know how I write my novels. They just seem to get done.

"Still nothing?" I asked Mort over the phone. It was the morning of my seminar.

"Nope, Jess. Ice is a foot thick on the river. Got a foot of snow on top of that. Afraid we won't be making much progress till things warm up."

"I know how hard you're trying, Mort. Just thought I'd check in again."

"Always a pleasure hearin' from you, Jess, no matter what the reason."

I stood in front of a floor-length mirror in my bedroom, admiring my brown-and-beige plaid wool skirt, ivory cashmere turtleneck, and beige cashmere blazer. I said aloud, "I'm delighted to see everyone here this morning."

I shifted my pose, extended my hands in front of me, and said, less enthusiastically, "How lovely to see you all on this frigid Maine morning. I'm especially excited because it's always a delight to spend an entire daytime with so many who share something in common—an interest in writing."

My smile was forced, false. I felt like a beauty pageant contestant with Vaseline smeared over her teeth. Relax, I told myself. Be yourself. You're in control. They'll be hanging on every word. You don't have to put on a show. Just talk about what you know. Be sincere. Use their questions as a basis for what to say next. Remember what FDR said: "The only thing we have to fear is—"

The phone rang.

"Good morning, Jessica. Michael O'Neill."

"Good morning, Michael."

"Getting ready for your seminar?"

"Oh, that? Haven't had a minute to even think about it."

"Spoken like a real pro. Good news. Your seminar is sold-out."

"Pardon?"

"It's sold-out. Not another seat available."

"I'm sorry, Michael, but I don't understand. I thought I was lecturing to artists-in-residence at Worrell."

"Oh, but you are. The resident artists, plus those from outside who wish to avail themselves of your considerable experience and talent. Didn't you see the ad?"

"No."

"No matter. It would have been a shame to limit your seminar to the few writers here at the institute. You have quite a following. We even advertised in Boston. Quite a contingent signed up from there."

"I—I'll do my best."

"Which will be far more than anyone can hope for. Need a ride? I'll send a car."

"No need. Jake's Cab Company is on its way."

"See you then."

Our conversation over, I poured another cup of coffee and pondered the day. Amazing, I thought, how life goes on even when life has been taken.

It had only been a few days since Dr. Meti's BMW, and the note allegedly written by Norm Huffaker, had been found at Moose River. A goodnight's sleep had eluded me ever since. I would wake up with intense, Technicolor visions of his body encased in ice beneath the river's surface, grotesquely configured, arms and legs twisted into awkward directions, his face—that face I knew so well—frozen into a macabre expression. Were his eyes open? Had the river's cold made it easier to die? They say that of all the ways for wild animals to die, freezing to death was the most painless and merciful. Had Norm frozen? Or had he drowned? Undoubtedly the latter.

If he'd gone into the river at all.

I had to admit that with every passing hour, the likelihood of his being dead was increased exponentially. If he was alive, where was he? Why no phone call? To me. Certainly to his wife.

My last conversation with Jill had been late last night. I'd called her at midnight my time, which made it nine o'clock in Los Angeles. Our conversation reflected a pattern Jill seemed to have fallen into ever since I broke the news to her. She was becoming increasingly resigned to Norman being dead.

She even talked of making funeral arrangements, a memorial service in Hollywood at which his many friends and colleagues in the movie business could pay their respects.

"Isn't that a little premature?" I suggested. "Somehow, Jill, I—"

"No, Jess," she said. "As much as I want to be optimistic, I'm afraid it's time for reality to be let in the door. The reality is that Norman is gone. Dead. Frozen beneath that river. I've finally come to grips with it. That's healthy."

"I suppose so," I said. "But give it a little more time. Maybe you should plan to come here."

"I've thought a lot about that," she said. "But I think you were right in suggesting I stay in California. Not because I'm waiting for a call from Norm any longer. But this is home, Jess. It was home for both of us."

"I'm sure you're right," I said. "Probably academic anyway. I just heard on the radio that the airport at Bangor is still closed. They're hoping to open it for limited flights by tomorrow. We got twenty-five inches."

It was good to hear her laugh. "You just confirmed my decision to stay put," she said.

And that's how we ended our talk.

I'd packed my briefcase the previous night with everything I thought I'd need for the seminar. But I checked it again that morning. There was a lesson plan of sorts, which included points I didn't want to forget to bring up. I packed copies of some of my novels to distribute; O'Neill's announcement that the crowd would be large meant that most aspiring writers in it would not receive them.

I'd also prepared a list of writers' associations to distribute. The writer's world can be lonely. Having the opportunity to join other writers for lunch, or an occasional cocktail, can be therapeutic, a surrogate employee cafeteria.

I included several drafts of my most recent novel, replete with my careful, copious pencil edits as an example of one of two favorite sayings about writing: All good writing is rewriting.

The other is: If I had more time, I would have written less.

I kept adding to the briefcase. I tossed in what I consider to be the "Bible" of style, punctuation, and grammar these days, the *Chicago Manual of Style*. I also decided to include in my bag of tricks a copy of *Gin and Daggers,* a novel written by a dear and departed friend, Marjorie Ainsworth, who was considered by many to be the world's reigning queen of the mystery novel. I'd been a houseguest at her London mansion the weekend she was murdered. Months following that, I received in the mail from her solicitor the original manuscript of *Gin and Daggers,* which Marjorie had willed to me. The note from her attorney that accompanied the manuscript enjoys a special, framed spot in my office: *"The torch has been passed. Ms. Ainsworth often said she considered you her favorite colleague, and wanted very much for you to possess this."*

As I pulled *Gin and Daggers* from the shelf, my eyes focused on two novels that stood next to it. As part of my compulsive nature, my bookshelves are carefully arranged by category, including a large selection devoted to books written by friends, and inscribed to me. Norman Huffaker's two early western novels, *The Redemption of Rio Red*, and *The Bronze Lady of Bentonville*, written under his pseudonym, B. K. Praether, were included in that collection. I placed them in the briefcase, too. I could use all the props I could muster. Norm's books would allow me to open a discussion of why writers are often compelled to write under different names, usually because certain books marked a drastic departure from the style for which they were well-known. And, of course, when ghostwriting a book for someone else demanded the author's anonymity.

I checked the wall clock. I still had time before Jake arrived, and took my coffee into my den where I'd placed Norm's computer, and other belongings, in a closet. I opened the computer carrying case. Secured inside by a Velcro strap was the computer itself, a marvel of miniaturization. A marvel to me, at least. My word processor was large. The keyboard was full-sized, and the monitor took up considerable desk space. But here was everything in a small package.

I removed the computer, pressed on a latch, and raised the screen, which was hinged to the body. I knew a laptop computer contained batteries, which meant I could probably turn it on without plugging it in. Dare I try? My computer illiteracy had me in a firm grip. I wasn't sure what would happen if I hit the "ON" button. Everything erased from the internal disk? Smoke and flames?

I turned it on. A light flashed. I leaned closer and read the writing just below the light. "LOW BATTERY."

I fished through an outside pocket of the case and pulled out an AC cord, found the tiny extrusion into which one end was plugged, and inserted the other end into a wall socket. After a few beeps, and a barrage of technical information that flashed across the screen, a brightly colored mosaic informed me I had entered the world of something called "WINDOWS."

"My goodness," I said.

A tiny arrow sat between two of many icons on the screen. That, I knew, had to be moved to one of the icons if anything were to happen. But how to move it?

A mouse. I'd played with computer mice (is that the correct plural in computerese?) before on a friend's computer.

More digging through another outside pocket produced what I assumed was this computer's version of a mouse. It had a little ball on top. I squinted to read the labels above inputs at the rear of the computer, found the one for the mouse, and plugged it in. My thumb went into spasm as I tried to roll the ball in such a way that it would direct the small screen arrow to the icon that said "MICROSOFT WORD," which I assumed was the writing program Norm used.

Eventually, I succeeded. I clicked a button on the side of the ball's housing. Nothing. I tried a few more times with the same negative result. Then, inadvertently, I clicked twice on it, and everything changed on the screen. It became blank, with only a blinking cursor.

I was trying to figure out how to access the internal disk when there was a loud knock at my door. I went to it and faced Jake Monroe.

"Is it time?" I asked.

"Yes, ma'am."

"Come in, Jake. Only be a minute. I have to turn off the computer."

"Gettin' fancy," he said.

"I suppose so. Pour yourself some coffee. It's in the carafe in the kitchen."

I was sure there were rules to follow when turning off the laptop, but I didn't know them. I simply touched the power button, hoping it wouldn't hurt the machine. I grabbed my briefcase, put on my L.L. Bean parka and duck boots, and was off to the Worrell Institute for Creativity.

"Good morning everyone," I said, "and welcome to the Worrell Institute for Creativity. I must admit that when Dr. O'Neill informed me that many of you would be from outside the institute, I suffered a momentary panic. But I think we'll all adjust just fine, and that you'll take away from today some useful information about writing a murder mystery."

I felt surprisingly relaxed. As O'Neill was introducing me, I remembered the advice of an old friend who made a living giving lectures and speeches. "Just pretend everyone in the audience is naked," he'd said.

Which I did, but only for an initial minute. The large room was cold. Obviously, the extensive renovations on the Worrell Mansion hadn't included an upgrading of the building's central heating system. Pretend everyone in the room was naked? The only visual I could come up with was a convention of goose pimples. I replaced everyone's clothing and relied on my own inner ability to stay calm.

"Let me begin by reminding you of one simple truth: 'The art of writing is the art of applying the seat of the pants to the seat of the chair.'"

The quote got the response I'd hoped for. They laughed. I was becoming more relaxed by the minute.

"I'm afraid I can't take credit for that clever comment," I said. "An American writer named Mary Heaton Vorse said it many years ago, and it's as applicable today as it was back then. It applies to all writers—mystery writers, novelists, non-fiction writers, speech writers, and poets."

There were nods throughout the room.

"Another saying that I often recall when preparing to sit down and write, was quipped by the famous, and impish Noel Coward. He said, 'What I adore is supreme professionalism. I'm bored by writers who can write only when it is raining.'"

"To that, I say, in the vernacular, 'Right on!' Many men and women who call themselves writers wait for a rainy night, or another externally induced mood, to write. Everything must be right. The setting must be right. The weather must be right. Well, I consider that not only nonsense, it represents, at least to me, a cop-out, to use another popular term. Professional writers—*real* writers—don't wait for rainy days and nights, although I'm sure Mr. Coward had plenty of those in England."

There was more laughter. This was easier than I'd anticipated, made more so by familiar faces in the crowd. Susan Dalton, whose aspirations to write a mystery had been clearly spelled out to me, sat front and center. Jo Jo Masarowski, the computer artist, was next to her. What he would get out of a lecture on mystery writing was beyond me.

But he wasn't the only nonwriter in the audience. Barbara McCoy, the musician who'd accused Maureen Beaumont of having stolen her musical score, was in the third row.

It occurred to me during O'Neill's introduction that the outsiders had paid to be here. How much it had cost them, I didn't know. Obviously, O'Neill and his staff saw the seminar as a moneymaking opportunity. I couldn't blame them for that. O'Neill had insisted I accept a token payment. We'd settled on a hundred dollars, which I intended to contribute to the children's wing of our local hospital. I just wished he'd been more forthright. Keeping it to himself until the last minute had left me with a slightly salty taste.

I'd just gotten into the subject of plotting when a serious, and overtly nervous young man, interrupted with a question.

"Go ahead," I said. "I intended to have a formal question-and-answer period later. But let's open it up now. Fire away when a question hits you."

A woman interrupted the young man. "It's freezing in here," she said, wrapping her arms around herself for emphasis.

"It is cold," I said. "I suggest everyone put their coats back on."

"They can't pay the heating bill?" an elderly gentleman muttered.

I buttoned my cardigan sweater and pointed to the young man with the question. "Maybe we can heat things up with some provocative questions," I said.

He introduced himself as a struggling mystery writer, who didn't depend upon his imagination to come up with titillating plots. He preferred to turn to newspapers and news magazines to provide him with juicy characters, and twists of plot.

I smiled. "Certainly," I said, "the novelist's imagination often pales in comparison to real life, especially in these days of Lorena Bobbits and Joey Butafuccos. But what it means to me is that the novelist must simply work harder to compete with life's crazy real events."

I suggested a fifteen-minute break. I'd been talking for over an hour. And, I needed a bathroom. Too much of Seth's coffee that morning.

I quickly left the makeshift stage, beat the crowd out the door of the conference room, and was on my way down the stairs when Michael O'Neill stopped me. "How is it going?" he asked.

"Fine. I think."

"I haven't been able to sit in yet. Hopefully this afternoon, after lunch. From the sounds of the applause, I'd say you have them in the palm of your hand."

"It's going smoothly."

"Got a moment?"

"Just one. Nature is calling."

He grinned. "Just one, Jessica. Promise. Amanda and I are getting a divorce."

"I'm sorry to hear that Michael." I didn't add that it came as no surprise."

"It's messy. Getting messier by the moment."

"These things sometimes are. Excuse me. I really have to—"

"Jessica."

"Yes?"

"Are you free for dinner this evening?"

"Uh, yes. No. I have plans. Excuse me."

I escaped to the restroom.

"Mrs. Fletcher."

Barbara McCoy followed me through the door. "I'm enjoying this so much," she said.

"Glad you could make it, Barbara."

"You're an amazing woman, Mrs. Fletcher. Jessica. It must be so hard for you to focus on anything other than Norman's disappearance. You were such good friends."

Disappearance? Not death? Her choice of words surprised me.

"Yes," I answered. "It does preoccupy my thoughts

at times. But, as they say, the show must go on. Speaking of that."

I emerged from my stall. Barbara was waiting. We left the restroom together.

"Barbara, when was the last time you saw Norm Huffaker?" I asked as we went up the stairs.

"Monday. We had breakfast together."

"You used the word 'disappearance.' I take from that you have doubts about whether he took his life. Any idea where he might have gone? Did he say anything at breakfast that morning?"

"Not a clue. That's what's so mysterious about it. That note found in Dr. Meti's car. I don't buy it. Norman was not suicidal!"

She evidently knew Norm better than I'd realized.

"Maybe he was kidnapped," she said. "Or he's no longer Norman Huffaker."

"Meaning?"

"Maybe he's assumed a new identity, is living off the land in Wisconsin. Or Brazil."

With another woman? I mused. Mort Metzger had raised that possibility.

"Barbara, do you have any evidence to support what you're suggesting?"

"No. Just a gut instinct, which I always trust."

"I hope your gut is right this time," I said. "Time for me to get back."

The rest of the morning flew by. I stressed the need for revision and rewrite. "You can't rewrite enough," I said. I passed out copies of the manuscript I'd brought, as well as the published book.

"Compare the first few pages of the first draft of the manuscript with the finished pages in the book," I said. "You'll see that the published product bears little resemblance to the draft."

I ended the morning session with a reminder that one of the cardinal sins of fiction writing is to tell the reader what a character is all about, rather than allowing the character to evolve through his or her actions. "Play out a scene. Don't *tell* the reader what has happened. Let readers experience it, and come to the conclusion you intend for them to reach. Describe a beautiful woman—what she wears, how she holds herself—rather than *saying* she's beautiful. I once asked a friend of mine, a wonderful composer of popular music, to write a song for me. His response was, 'If you told me to write a love song tonight, I'd have a lot of trouble doing it. But if you tell me to write a love song about a girl in a red dress in a bar, who's on her fifth martini, and whose lover is dancing close to another woman while red-dress is falling off her chair, that makes it a lot easier.' "

Pleased with the way the morning had gone, I announced that the institute had prepared a delicious lunch for everyone attending the seminar. "Before we fill our stomachs," I said, "I'll take a few questions about what's been discussed this morning."

The room resembled a baseball stadium filled with fans doing "the wave." Everyone seemed to have a question.

"Do you have favorite mystery writers?" I was asked.

"Oh, yes. Many." I talked a little about Marjorie Ainsworth. "But there are so many others," I said. "I'm as much of a fan of Ruth Rendell and P. D. James as I'm sure most of you are. But don't limit your reading to only the most popular authors, or those of most recent vintage. Poe and Dickens wrote superb mysteries. And, of course, Dame Christie. I love Dorothy Sayers. Read Wilkie Collins, especially his classic, 'Woman in White.' Stanley Ellin. Margaret Millar. Recently, I've been reading everything I can get my hands on by Ellis Peters. Mixing history and murder is so much fun. Next?"

I pointed to a middle-aged woman whose red hair was swept up in a French bun, and whose sequined aqua blouse had caught my attention earlier.

"Mrs. Fletcher, my name is Audrey Black. I'm with the *Boston Globe*. You were a close friend of Norman Huffaker. Could you comment on the recent rash of suicides that have occurred here at Worrell?"

I was momentarily speechless. A reporter at the seminar, whose only interest was gaining a quote for a story?

"Ms. Black," I said, "I admit my surprise at your question. I must also tell you that I will not answer it. I will only take questions about the subject of this seminar."

"All right," she said. "How has the suicide of Norman Huffaker impacted the novel you're currently working on?"

"Another question?" I asked, scanning the room, and avoiding the *Globe* reporter.

I acknowledged an older gentleman with a shock of thin gray hair, and a scraggly gray beard. "Yes, sir?"

"Mrs. Fletcher, wouldn't you say that what's taken place here at Worrell in the last few weeks is the stuff that dreams are made of for mystery writers?"

"Perhaps."

"The earlier discussion about building plots and characters from real life intrigued me," he said. "Surely, it's crossed your mind that a potentially Edgar-winning plot is unfolding right before your eyes."

"I haven't thought of it that way," I said. Which was true. While I use all of my life experiences in writing my novels, the unfortunate incidents at Worrell had not become grist for any writing I would do, even though I was using a similar artists' retreat as a setting for *Brandy & Bullets*.

But he had a point.

"I suppose you could perceive the tragic events here as a basis for a murder mystery out of the 'cozy' school," I said. "Artists' retreat. Professional jealousies." I looked at Barbara McCoy, who'd accused Maureen Beaumont of having stolen her musical score. Her face was blank. "Motive," I continued. "Proximity. Unstated agendas. Yes. Of course it makes for a potential plot. But so does a diner like Mara's in town. The mayor's office. The local hospital. No. I have not considered the events here at the

Worrel Institute to be fertile ground for any book I intend to write. One of the victims was a dear friend." I looked at Ms. Black from the Boston *Globe*. "I prefer to write about crimes that haven't been committed in real life, victims who are personally unknown to me. Thank you for your attention this morning. Lunch is served. Hopefully, the food will be warmer than this room has been."

Chapter Thirteen

I arrived home from Worrell at five, chilled to the bone. I turned up the electric heat in the house and crouched over one of the baseboard units, rubbing my hands and blowing on them. It was the kind of chill you only experience when exposed to low temperatures indoors for an extended period, a pervasive cold, different from being outdoors in winter. I seldom suffer from the cold in winter, but invariably start shivering when temperatures moderate in early spring. Must have to do with the humidity, or weather inversion, or something. My brief college flirtation with becoming a weather forecaster hadn't provided the answer.

I put a match to the newspapers, kindling, and logs I'd stacked in the fireplace before leaving that morning. The sheer sight of flames springing to life was immediately warming. My chill wasn't terminal. A hot buttered rum, and gravlax I'd prepared the night before, would complete my thaw.

I slipped my cold feet into big, bulky, fuzzy sheepskin slippers, set my rum and gravlax on a table next to my recliner in front of the fireplace, sat, stretched my legs, sighed contentedly, and reflected on the day.

The seminar had gone well, despite the intrusion of Ms. Black from the *Boston Globe,* and another reporter from a supermarket checkout tabloid who suggested that the Worrell Mansion might be haunted.

"Have you see any ghosts?" I'd asked.

"I can feel them," she said.

"Are they as cold as I am?" I asked, which brought a few snickers from the audience.

"You don't believe in ghosts?" she asked me.

"No, I don't. On the other hand, I don't *not* believe in them, any more than I summarily dismiss reports of UFOs. Do you have a question concerning the writing of a mystery novel?"

"Why are people dying here?"

"Without question, at the hand of a vindictive ghost," I said. "Let's get back to the business of plotting."

As I sat in my recliner, and sipped my rum, I realized how fatiguing the day had been. I was exhausted. Working all day in a cold environment hadn't helped. But my exhaustion had more to do with having to exercise my brain than with the temperature. People who don't spend their working days *thinking* have trouble understanding how tiring it can be. I always know when a day at my word processor has been successful. If I don't come away from it drained, it hasn't been.

I was asleep within minutes, aided and abetted by the demon rum that hit my stomach, and immediately radiated throughout my body.

"Damn!" I mumbled as the phone rang. "Hello."

"Jessica. It's Michael."

Your timing is atrocious. I've had enough of you and your dank, cold Worrell Institute for Creativity for one day. You woke me up.

"Hello, Michael," I said.

"Am I interrupting my newest professor in the middle of something profound?" he asked. "In the process of resolving a murder?"

"No, you're not." For reasons all my own, and unknown to me, I seldom admit to napping. "What can I do for you?" I asked.

"I wanted to congratulate you for a job exceedingly well-done, Jessica. Your seminar was a resounding success."

"Thank you."

"Everyone's talking about it. I sense a renewed spirit in the place. You provided inspiration and, may I add, generated some needed cash flow." He laughed.

"Happy to hear that. Might I suggest that you use some of that cash flow to boost the heat at Worrell? Or buy a space heater."

"Reason number two for my call. To apologize for the lack of heat. Heating this splendid mansion is next to impossible. I can see why Jared Worrell was anxious to unload it. At any rate, Jessica, I promise you that for your next seminar, you and your students will be warm as toast."

"That's good to hear." My eyes were heavy; I stifled a loud yawn.

"Reason number three for calling."

"Yes?"

"I was hoping to avail myself of the rain check you so graciously offered."

"Rain check?"

"Dinner. Just the two of us. To get to know each other better."

I didn't remember having offered any rain check the last time Michael O'Neill invited me for dinner. But maybe I had, as a polite thing to say when declining his invitation.

"Well? How about tonight? While the seminar is fresh in your mind."

"Impossible. I'm beat, Michael."

"Tomorrow night?"

"No. I'm about to go into my hibernation mode. I'm behind on my latest book. My publisher is putting on the pressure. I'm afraid I—"

His laugh was meant to be pacific. "I understand, Jessica. Pursuing a professional woman, especially one of your caliber, is never easy. But I'm patient. And persevering. You won't mind my putting some pressure of my own on, will you? Gently, of course. And never stepping over the boundary of good taste."

"No. That will be fine. Thanks for calling. I'm glad the seminar was a success."

I didn't wish to be rude, but he had crossed the line, in my estimation, between first-time offender to nuisance. Not that I would be critical of his wanting a dinner companion, now that he and his wife had decided to call it quits. But he'd have to look elsewhere for that companion. Frankly, I'd developed a slight dislike for Dr. Michael O'Neill. Nothing specific that he'd done or said. More a matter of being a little too slick, too self-assured, for my taste. I like men who are comfortable with who they are—as long as there is a parallel acknowledgment of their vulnerability.

I was too sleepy to ponder it further. I poked at the dwindling fire, added a few logs that brought it back to life, and went to the kitchen to replenish my hot buttered rum. On the way back, I paused at one of my bookshelves, the one on which books my friends were proudly displayed. One of Norm Huffaker's two western novels, which I'd replaced upon returning from the seminar, *The Bronze Lady of Bentonville,* caught my eye, as though beckoning me to choose it, and to pull it down from its perch.

Its cover was bold and colorful, with a beautiful Indian maiden watching two dashing men on horseback gallop toward her. Norm's nom de plume, B. K. Praether, was in large white letters.

I carried the book to my chair, opened it, and read his inscription to me: *"For Jessica—One step in hopefully becoming half the writer you are. Love. Norman."*

I suffered a twinge of guilt at never having read this particular book. I'd read his other western, *The Redemption of Rio Red,* and enjoyed it. There was a time early in my career when my attitude toward western novels was that they were a lesser genre, not for serious readers. Until, of course, I matured and realized that a good story is a good story, whether it's set in the old West, or contemporary Manhattan. Norm was a good storyteller. That he chose ten-gallon hats and spurs, rather than three-piece suits, for his characters was irrelevant.

It was during this intolerant, opinionated period of my life that I considered writers who wrote under pseudonyms to be cowardly, not willing to subject their real selves to the possibility of harsh criticism. Then, during a particularly productive year in which I turned out three books, my editor suggested publishing one under another name. "Too many books in too short a time by a single author can be counterproductive," he'd said.

And so Cynthia Syms was born. I felt in good company: Writing as Barbara Vine certainly hadn't done Ruth Rendell any harm. Nor had Evan Hunter suffered writing under his Ed McBain byline. Cynthia Syms's book didn't sell as well as those under my name. But years later, when it was reissued, the cover noted that it was J. B. Fletcher writing as Cynthia Syms. That edition did quite well.

I once asked Norman how he felt about not having his real name on a book. "As long as my real name is on the check," he'd replied. Hard to argue with that level of pragmatism.

As I browsed *The Bronze Lady of Bentonville,* I realized how good a writer Norm really was, even at that early stage of his career. The writing was tight, and spare. His characters were colorful and three-dimensional, his action scenes stirring. It was hard to imagine him dead; his writing was so alive.

My sleepiness had abandoned me. I was wide-awake. I added more logs to the fire, propped a yellow legal pad on my lap, and started making notes, beginning with the assumption that Norm was alive. If so, what might have really happened?

He went to the bridge, left the BMW idling, then departed the scene rather than jumping into the river.

Okay.

But how did he leave the scene?

Where did he go?

And why would he have done such a stupid thing?

Fifteen minutes later, Jake Monroe knocked at my front door. I was already dressed in my outdoor gear.

"Where to on this frigid night, Mrs. Fletcher?" he asked.

"Believe it or not, Jake, the Old Moose River Bridge."

Jake frowned. His heavy salt-and-pepper eyebrows formed question marks.

"I know, I know," I said. "Sorry. Hopefully, this will be the last time. I just have to check something out."

Jake nodded. "The Old Moose River Bridge it is," he said.

The road crews had done their usual splendid job of keeping the roads clear. We reached the bridge quickly. Jake and I got out and peered over its railing into the thick white mass below. Frozen. Everything was frozen, including my breath. Where there was once—and would be again—a strong current of clear, fresh water, there was now at least six inches of ice, with a blanket of snow on top. Spring was a long way off, especially in Maine, where it is preceded by what's known as Maine's "fifth season"—

mud season—and usually arrives a day or two before summer officially begins.

Hard to believe, I thought, my arms wrapped tightly about me, a stiff wind off the river stinging my nose and cheeks, that the frozen water would once again host white-water rafters, with their yellow float jackets and gleeful faces.

"Where do rafters in summer park their cars?" I asked no one in particular.

"Mostly down there," Jake answered, pointing in the direction of a small cleared area that could accommodate three, maybe four vehicles.

I allowed my mind to drift back to summer and the sight of rafters navigating the tricky currents of the river. Dozens of them. On some days even more.

"This is the starting point for white-water rafting, isn't it?" I asked.

"Ayuh. Most of 'em pick up the river here. Go all the way down to Fillerville. Them's that make it, that is."

I walked to the end of the narrow bridge and looked to a path that meandered down to a tiny beach of sorts at the river's edge. The rafters usually came down that path in order to enter the water. But where did they all park? Certainly not on the bridge itself. It accommodated only one car at a time in each direction.

I asked Jake.

He laughed. "Don't you remember all the flap about them parking over to Jimmy's Store Twenty-four? Jimmy raised a big stink about that. Tried to

band his parking lot, but they just kept findin' ways
to get around it."

"Yes, I remember now," I said.

Jimmy's Store 24 was a typical catch-all store:
bread, milk, magazines, and the like. When he first
started the business, Jimmy stayed open twenty-four
hours a day. But that didn't last long, especially in
winter. Now, he opened when the spirit struck him,
which on certain days—especially when he had an
"aidge-on" from too much whiskey—resulted in not
opening at all.

"How far would you say Jimmy's store is from
here?" I asked Jake.

" 'Bout a quarter mile."

"Not very far."

"That's for certain. That's why so many people
park there, even if they aren't buyin' from Jimmy's
store. That's what got him so upset. Remember?"

"Yes, I do. An easy walk from here, even in a
snowstorm."

My mind went into overdrive.

Suppose Norm was alive. Suppose he faked his
death, for reasons still unclear. How did he pull it
off? He could have left the BMW idling on the
bridge, then walked to Store 24 where he had someone waiting for him.

Another possibility presented itself to me as I
stood on the Old Moose River Bridge. Norm might
have been picked up after leaving the BMW. He
might have hitched a ride. Hitchhiking hadn't fallen
out of favor in Maine to the extent it had in other,
more urban parts of the country. Lots of locals pick

up anyone with a protruding thumb, provided the hitchhiker isn't foaming at the mouth, and carrying a submachine gun. In a sense, hitchhiking is the closest thing Cabot Cove has to mass transit.

But it was unlikely that someone would have been driving that night, especially down by the river.

Which meant that if Norm had been picked up, it could have been by prearrangement, in which case someone in Cabot Cove knew about it, and perhaps even knew where Norm had gone—and why.

"Jake," I said, "isn't there a gas station next to Store Twenty-four?"

"Ayuh."

"And a car rental agency that recently opened?"

"Right again, Mrs. Fletcher."

Maybe Norm rented a car there, I thought. If he did, he might have driven it to—an airport.

A sudden burst of frigid wind came up off the river, whipped around me, and came at my face with an icy slap. I gave myself a bear hug. "Let's go," I said.

"Back home?" Jake asked. It sounded more like a plea.

"No, not just yet. First, I need to stop off at Store Twenty-four for something. Okay?"

"Fine by me," he said. "I could use a cup of coffee."

"Sounds good," I said. "My treat."

"I need to check in on the agency anyway," he said.

"Check in? Agency?"

"Ayuh. Can't imagine business is much good in

dead of winter. Never should have bought into the franchise. Might sell my stake come spring."

"What stake? You've lost me." We'd climbed into his taxi.

"Rent-a-Wreck. The one by Jimmy's store. Bought into it just last summer."

"That's good to know," I said, smiling.

"Why? You don't drive, Mrs. F."

"I didn't realize you needed to know how to drive when you rent a wreck," I said.

Jake laughed. "You've got a good point there," he said. "Let's get that coffee."

We were served by a surly young woman manning Jimmy's store, and took our cups into the office of Rent-a-Wreck. It was closed. How fortunate that Jake owned a piece of it, and had a key.

He turned on the lights. It was as cold inside as it was out. Jake flipped a switch on a floor heater. "Should get livable in a couple of minutes," he said.

"Don't worry about it," I said. "I'm used to it."

"What now, Mrs. F?"

"I'd like to see your rental records for the day the blizzard hit. The day Norman Huffaker disappeared." I gave him the date.

"Suppose I can find those records," he said. "Not sure where to look. Don't pay much attention to what goes on here, 'cept for whether it made any money. Hasn't lately." He started rummaging through dog-eared boxes of files. "Never cared how things worked here. Like I said, I was hopin' it would help me and the Mrs. retire someday."

"I'm looking for a rental to Norman Huffaker." I spelled his name.

"Gottcha."

"And it's between us," I said. "Whatever we come up with."

"Gottcha, Mrs. F."

After a few more minutes of pulling pieces of paper from the files, Jake held up a batch. "These here are from that day," he said. "Let's see. Huffaker. Huffaker." He perused each rental receipt. "Nope. I don't see anybody with that name, for that day. Only rented eleven. Looks like I'd better count on drivin' instead of retiring."

"Could I take a look myself?" I asked.

"Sure can. Hope you have more luck than me."

I flipped through each rental agreement with my index finger, like an Evelyn Wood speed-reader. The records were dirty, smudged, dog-eared. Some names were virtually illegible.

No Norman Huffaker.

But then during a second run, my finger stopped, as if the agreement were written in braille.

Praether.

B. K. Praether.

Red Chevy.

Norman, the ghost, a.k.a. B. K. Praether.

"Gorry, what brings you here this time of night, young lady?"

"Sorry to barge in on you, Mort. Let's just say that I was in the neighborhood."

Mort peered at me over the rim of half-glasses,

which he usually wears only at night, and at home. We all have our pockets of vanity. Wearing glasses is one of our sheriff's.

"Hope I'm not interrupting anything," I said.

"Nothin' that can't wait. I've been trying to come up with new rules for my game. Parker Brothers still doesn't like the old ones."

Mort had spent the past few years fine-tuning a board game he'd invented. It was a murder mystery game. He'd sent it to the large game company, Parker Brothers, and anxiously awaited its response, like an author sending off a first novel and checking the mail six times a day.

"I'm sure you'll work it out," I said. "I was just down at the Old Moose River Bridge."

"In this weather. Below zero down there, I figure."

"It was cold. Jake Monroe took me. I had him drop me off here. He left to pick up someone. He'll be back in a half hour."

"What were you doin' down at the bridge?"

"Brainstorming, actually."

"Seems more sensible doing that in front of a fireplace."

"I thought the same thing. I found something very important, Mort."

"Don't tell me you found Norman's body."

"No. Thank God. But I did find a body of evidence."

"Take off your coat and sit awhile, Jess. I'm all ears."

I spoke while taking off my hat, scarf, and other layers of winter clothing. "I happened to go to the

Rent-a-Wreck car rental agency. You know the one. By Jimmy's Store Twenty-four. By the bridge."

"I get it," he said. "Mr. Norman Huffaker rented a car there. Right?"

"Wrong."

He sighed, crossed his arms, and shook his head. "Don't keep me in suspense, Jess. Save that for your readers."

"B. K. Praether rented a car from the agency the day before Norm's alleged suicide note was found."

"Who the hell is B. J. Praether?"

"B. K. Praether."

"What's this Praether fella have to do with Huffaker?"

"He's Norman's ghost."

"Uh-huh. You feelin' okay?"

"I feel a lot better knowing what I now know."

"And what you now know, it seems to me, is that Norman Huffaker is dead, but his ghost rented a car from Rent-a-Wreck."

"Exactly. A red Chevrolet. Only Norman isn't dead. I'd bet my life on it."

"That's bein' pretty sure, Jess."

"Norm faked his suicide at the bridge, walked to the Rent-a-Wreck agency, got in his rented Chevy, and drove to—"

"I'm listening."

"Drove to an airport. Bangor. Boston. Maybe even West Hartford."

"In that storm?"

"Yes. What I need for you to do is to put an all-points on the rented car he used. Here." I handed him a photocopy of the rental receipt. "All the airports he might have reached before they shut down."

"Jessica, I've got a reputation of sorts to keep. I'm not about to put out an all-points for a ghost's car."

I laughed. "Ghostwriter," I said. "Praether is the pen name Norman used early in his career. He wrote two western novels under it."

"Oh. Now I get it. All right. I'll put out the bulletin right away."

"Thanks, Mort."

Jake arrived. I put on my coat and hat, thanked Mort again, and headed for home.

"Accomplish what you were after?" Jake asked.

"I certainly did, Jake. And it wouldn't have been possible without you."

He grinned. "That's always good to hear, Mrs. F. Looks like me buyin' into that Rent-a-Wreck agency paid off, at least for you."

"Yes, it did, Jake."

"Just wish it'd make some money."

"It will," I said. "Give it time. Everything takes time."

"Jess. Mort here. Sorry to be calling so late, but thought you'd want to know as soon as I got word. B. K. Praether flew from Boston to Washington, D.C. Dumped that red Chevy in the long-term lot at Logan. Must've been a hell of a ride in that storm. At any rate, your dead friend—at least his ghost—is in our nation's capital."

I sat up in bed to confirm I wasn't in a deep REM sleep. "Washington? I wonder why he went there."

"Can't answer that, Mrs. F. 'Course, he's a writer. You know how *they* are." He chuckled.

"I can't thank you enough, Mort. You sound exhausted. Get some rest."

"Exactly what I intend to do. Good night."

I looked at the clock. One-thirty. Ten-thirty in Los Angeles.

I called from my office downstairs. Jill answered on the first ring.

"Hello, Jill. It's Jessica."

"I know," she said.

"You do? Expecting a call from me?"

"No. I just had Caller ID installed. When the phone rings, you see the phone number of the person calling you. It's a wonderful feature."

"So I've heard. Did you get it in the hope that Norman might call, and it would help you track him down?"

"Of course not, Jessica. Norman is dead. I've accepted that. I think it's time everyone did, including you, my good friend. What are you doing up so late? You were always an early-to-bed, early-to-rise person."

"I'm wide-awake, Jill, because I have exciting news for you. Norman didn't jump from that bridge. He's alive."

"What?"

"I tracked him down through a car-rental agency in town. He rented a red Chevy from a place called Rent-a-Wreck, the day before he left his so-called suicide note. He drove to Boston that night, and flew out of there to Washington, D.C."

There was silence on the other end.

"Maybe there are two Norman Huffakers," she suggested.

"But only one B. K. Praether. He signed the rental agreement using his pseudonym, Jill."

"That's—that's far-fetched, Jess. Sorry, but I don't buy it. Why would he fly to Washington? Besides, if Norm were alive, he'd call me. He wouldn't put me through this. You know that. If my husband were alive, he'd call. He's never tried to cause me pain. This would be the most extreme form of cruelty. Norman isn't capable of that. Of committing suicide? Yes. Of hiding from me? No."

Discussing it any further was futile. She'd finally accepted her husband's death. That was hard enough. Now, with my news, she'd have to go through another process that she wasn't ready for. And who could blame her? It hadn't occurred to me that her reaction would be anything but ecstatic. That was my problem. She needed time to digest what I'd said.

"Jess, someone is playing a nasty trick," she said. "Someone's trying to pretend that Norm didn't commit suicide. That's the only plausible answer." Her tone was firm and deliberate.

"I'm sorry, Jill. I know this is difficult for you."

"Oh, God," she sighed. "Jess, forgive me for sounding like a snapping turtle. I'm not angry with you. You've been wonderful, there for me every step of the way. Your heart's always been in the right place. Maybe I'm just angry at the world right now. Next time I'm in this mood, and see that it's your number on my Caller ID, I'll spare you my mood by not picking up."

"And I'd feel horrible if you did that. You don't have to spare me anything. I'll check in with you tomorrow, Jill. Try to get some sleep."

"You, too. Jess. And keep looking for Norman, on the outside chance you're right. I hope you are."

"You know I will. Good night, Jill."

Chapter Fourteen

I intended to indulge myself by sleeping a little later that morning. But Sheriff Mort Metzger's call at seven dashed that intention.

"Is this Jessica Fletcher, the famous mystery writer and public speaker?"

"Good morning, Mort."

"I figured you were up."

"You figured wrong. But I am now. Up. What can I do for you?" I knew he wanted something from me. There's a tone that creeps into his voice whenever he seeks a favor. That tone was there loud and clear.

"The pleasure of your company at breakfast, ma'am." He said it with an exaggerated cowboy twang.

Now I knew for certain he wanted something. No free lunches. Or breakfasts.

"Pick you up in half an hour?"

"An hour."

"Be there in forty-five minutes. We'll go to Mara's. I'll make a reservation."

"Mara doesn't take reservations."

"She will if I make it under your name. Your name's got clout in this town."

"Whatever you say. A stack of Mara's blueberry pancakes is suddenly appealing."

I was surprised, and pleased, to see Seth Hazlitt arrive with Mort in his patrol car. I hadn't spoken with him for a few days, not even on the phone.

"Good morning, Jessica," Seth said. "Been a stranger lately."

"I might say the same about you."

"Been busy. Delivered Sally James's baby early this mornin'. Fine-looking boy."

"Wonderful. Are you joining us for breakfast?"

"Ayuh. Never turn down a free meal from our sheriff."

As we stopped at an intersection with stop signs for all, a tan Jeep with Massachusetts plates ignored its sign and barreled through.

"Damn fool," Mort said, turning on his siren and flashing lights, and taking pursuit. The Jeep's driver, a young blond woman, quickly pulled over. Mort got out and sauntered up to her. Seth and I watched as the woman opened her door and joined Mort on the side of the road.

"Just like a woman," Seth said. The driver had begun to cry.

"Hardly a gender issue," I said.

"Look there, Jessica. She's pleading with him not to give her a ticket. Probably tellin' him she's got a sick and dying mother at the hospital, or a needy child at home."

Mort calmly wrote her a ticket. As he did, her tears turned to fury. We couldn't hear, but the words coming from her mouth were obviously not flattering to Mort.

When Mort rejoined us, Seth said, "Looks like whatever the young lady said, it didn't work."

"Said she had a sick mother, and a kid at home."

Seth smiled at me.

"What were her parting words?" I asked.

"Not fit for your ears, Jess. Sorry for the delay. She really worked up an appetite in me. Everybody hungry?"

"Ayuh," Seth said.

"Ayuh," I said.

Mara's was as busy and festive as usual. A temporary thaw had arrived in Cabot Cove; everyone seemed to have taken advantage of it by getting out of their homes. You grab those opportunities in a snowy place like Maine. Chances were good that any moderation in temperature wouldn't last long. I'd checked the local radio station before leaving my house. More blizzard-like weather was forecast for early evening.

The windows in Mara's were fogged from the heat. The heavy, pleasant aroma of fresh-brewed coffee and freshly baked cinnamon buns permeated the air. Mara had set aside a table for us, which undoubtedly annoyed the dozen people waiting for tables. I would have been content to join them, and wait my turn. But Mort had this thing about reservations. He viewed his ability to reserve tables in busy places as a perk of being chief law enforcement officer. He wasn't an arrogant man, but when it came to getting a table—

We ordered, and made small talk. I knew Mort would eventually announce why he'd arranged for us to have breakfast together. That was another quirk of our sheriff. He enjoyed leaving friends in suspense until he decided he was ready to communicate.

Mara placed my pancakes in front of me. A heaping mound of corned-beef hash arrived for Mort. Seth opted for oatmeal, eggs over-easy, a double side order of bacon, and an English muffin. Seth may be a physician, but he's never prescribed himself a low-fat diet.

"Delicious," I announced. "Now, Mort, what's behind this sudden, but admittedly pleasant, breakfast?" I looked to Seth, who shrugged, and consumed another tablespoon of oatmeal.

Mort grinned.

"What is it, Mort?"

"Looks like a hearty stack of blueberry pancakes to me," he said.

I guess my face mirrored my annoyance at being played with, because he added, "Dr. Michael O'Neill called me."

"And?"

"He wanted to know your favorite restaurant."

"Did he?"

"Yup."

"And why might he have done that?" I turned to my pancakes to indicate a lack of interest in the answer.

"Because he wants to take you to a real nice place."

"You've been seeing O'Neill?" Seth asked.

"Seeing him? No. Of course not."

"Seems to me he's smitten with you, Jessica," said Seth.

"He and his wife's gettin' a divorce," Mort said.

"Not a bad-looking fella," Seth said.

"Wanted to know other things about you, Jess," Mort said. "He asked me what kind of flowers you liked best. And whether you were partial to perfume, or chocolates."

"This is absurd," I said. "What restaurant did you tell him was my favorite?"

"Mara's," Mort said, giggling.

"At least you got that right," I said. I glanced about the busy luncheonette. No one seemed to be listening to us. I leaned across the small table and said to Mort, "Michael O'Neill has asked me to dinner twice. And twice I've turned him down." I added syrup to what was left of my stack. "Now, could we change the subject? Anything new with Norman? Anything from Washington?"

"I think you should go," Mort said.

"What about Norman?" Seth asked.

"I'll fill you in later."

"You find his body?" Seth asked Mort.

"I think you should go, Jess," Mort repeated.

"Don't think the thought hasn't occurred to me," I said. "I have friends in Washington I haven't seen for ages."

"I don't mean you should go to Washington," Mort said. "I think you should go to dinner with O'Neill."

"Does it count for anything that I have absolutely no interest in having dinner with Michael O'Neill? I prefer curling up with a good book in front of the fire instead of wasting time—his and mine."

"Case closed," said Seth, wiping his mouth with a napkin, sitting back, folding his hands over his corpulent belly, and smiling. "I never did like O'Neill much. Just proves that Jessica Fletcher's got good taste—in everything—especially men."

"Thank you, Doctor," I said.

"I'm not done yet," Mort said as Mara refilled our cups.

"I think you are," I said.

"Hear me out?" our sheriff asked.

"I always hear you out," I said.

Mort, too, checked the other customers. Secure that our conversation wouldn't go further than the table, he whispered to me, "Ever consider, Jessica, that having a simple dinner alone with O'Neill might turn up some useful information about your friend, Huffaker?"

Seth sat up straight. "What's goin' on with Norman Huffaker?"

"Later," I said, gently placing my index finger on Seth's lips. To Mort: "Go on. I'm listening."

"Seems to me, Jess, that whatever happened to your friend, and to the other victims—Miss Beaumont, who's dead, and the gal recovering in the hospital—this Worrell Institute's got something to do with it. You know I've never bought any of the official explanations. Still consider everything an open case."

"Yes, I know that."

"Dr. O'Neill runs that institute."

"Right."

"So, it strikes this cop that if anybody knows what's goin' on, it would be the boss. Dr. O'Neill."

"Makes sense," Seth said, anxious to be brought into the loop.

I didn't need any further explanation from Mort as to what he wanted me to do. I said, "You want me to go to dinner with Michael O'Neill on a ruse, under false pretenses, in order to coax information from him."

"Is that what you want her to do?" Seth asked Mort.

"Not a bad idea," Mort said. "Just dinner. Could clear up a lot of unanswered questions about your friend."

"I won't go to dinner on that basis," I said.

"Even if it would solve a murder?"

Would it? I silently asked myself.

"You're asking one of the most honest women I know to lie," Seth said.

"Not lie," Mort said. "Play-act a little. Nobody gets hurt."

"It would lead O'Neill on," Seth said. "Make him think Jessica has feelings for him."

"Just 'cause she accepts a dinner invitation? Nah. Just a dinner. What say, Jess? Could be real helpful."

"I suppose—"

"Now, hold on here a second," Seth said. "I don't

know what's going on with the disappearance of your friend, Huffaker, but did it ever occur to either of you that O'Neill might be askin' Jessica out to dinner so that *he* can find out what *she* knows?"

Seth's challenge brought conversation to a halt. Mort and I looked at each other. We both were influenced by Seth's comment. But our reactions were different. Mort was about to back off on his suggestion that O'Neill and I have dinner together.

For me, it gave me incentive to go through with it. If O'Neill was asking me to dinner in order to pump me, he had something to hide.

"Okay," I said. "I'll have dinner with Dr. Michael O'Neill, director of the Worrell Institute."

"You will?"

"Did you really tell Michael that Mara's was my favorite restaurant?" I asked.

"No. I told him you liked Le Poisson."

"As a matter of fact, I do," I said brightly. "Have to get back. I'm having guests for lunch."

I smelled fire. I ran into each room in search of smoke.

The doorbell rang.

"Not the clam pies," I shouted to my empty living room. I'd put the pies in the oven over an hour ago, and had forgotten about them.

"In a minute," I yelled at the front door as I headed for the kitchen. The pies were burned. Hopefully, some selective scraping would salvage them for lunch.

Jason and Jo Jo Masarowski stood at the door

when I opened it. I'd invited them for lunch for two reasons. First, I wanted to further nurture the friendship they'd evidently developed since Thanksgiving. Jason needed a friend, and Jo Jo had filled that role. They shared a love of computers, something I never would have thought possible with Jason. Just goes to show that beneath an otherwise uninspired exterior can lurk intelligence that simply needs to be unleashed. Computers—and Jo Jo—had done that.

My second reason for inviting them was less altruistic. I needed Jo Jo's computer expertise to bring up Norm's disks on his laptop computer. Try as I had, I'd been unsuccessful.

"Come in, come in," I said. The thaw was already giving way to colder, damper air. The sun had been shining earlier that morning. Now, the sky was an ominous gray, sinking lower with each passing hour. Another foot of snow was predicted to begin about eight, followed by freezing rain.

"Come in and warm yourselves up."

"Smells like fire, Mrs. F.," Jason said as they stepped into my foyer.

"Just our lunch," I said. "I'm afraid the clam pies I planned to serve have burned. But I might be able to resurrect them. If not, there's a big container of clam chowder in the freezer, and some fresh, crusty bread I picked up this morning from Sassi's. You won't go away hungry."

I led them into the kitchen where I'd set the table. "I think we'll go with the chowder," I said, casting a disappointed eye at the blackened pies sitting on the counter. "And a salad. Take but a minute."

"Can we help?" Jo Jo asked.

"No, thank you. Hard to burn soup. Just make yourselves at home."

"Gonna need me to shovel again tomorrow morning, Mrs. Fletcher," said Jason.

"Afraid so. It's quite a storm they're predicting. I don't know what I'd do without you, Jason."

Jason seemed pleased with himself, and looked to Jo Jo to be sure he'd heard my compliment. Jo Jo, it seemed to me, had assumed the role of a big brother to Jason. It was nice to see.

"Jessica, you mentioned something about computer problems," Jo Jo said. "Mind if I take a look before lunch?"

"Good idea," I said. "Let's go."

They eagerly followed me into my office. "Excuse the mess," I said, moving stacks of magazines off two chairs. "Before we get started, there's something I need to tell you. But it has to stay inside these four walls."

They nodded in agreement.

"What I have here is Norman Huffaker's computer, and disks that were with it. I want to pull up what's on those disks. I don't know whether the information on them will be helpful in learning what really happened to Norman. He was a very good friend of mine."

"I know that," Jo Jo said.

"Maybe—just maybe you'll find something for me that will put my mind at rest regarding his disappearance."

"You don't believe he jumped in the Moose River?" Jason asked.

"No, I don't."

"I don't, either," said Jo Jo.

"Well, then, let's hope you two geniuses can prove that."

I handed the disks to Jo Jo.

"No problem," he said, booting up the computer and inserting one of the disks into the drive. A directory of what was on that disk filled the screen. Four files were named: MEMO 1, MEMO 2, MEMO 3 and MEMORANDUM.

"Can we pull up each of those?" I asked.

"Sure," Jason said. "Show her, Jo Jo."

Who would Norman be writing memos to? I wondered. Memos usually involved interoffice communication. Norman worked in isolation, crafting his screenplays in a small, prefab cottage located at the far end of his sprawling property in Hollywood. Any correspondence on Norman's part would be in the form of a letter, not a memo.

Jo Jo brought MEMO 1 to the screen. It read: *"I'd like to hold a pep rally of sorts this afternoon to prepare us all for the opening of Worrell. Let's meet in my office at 3. Thanks. Michael."*

"This isn't from Norman," said Jason.

"Must be from Dr. O'Neill," I said. "Remember what I've asked of you. Don't tell anyone about these files."

"No problem, Mrs. Fletcher," Jason said.

MEMO 2: *"Sorry, guys. Have to reschedule today's pep*

*rally until tomorrow morning. Hope to see you all at
10 sharp. Donuts and coffee. Thanks. Michael."*

MEMO 3 was addressed to Beth Anne Portledge:
*"Kudos to you for a fine job of scheduling. Keep up the
good work. Michael."*

MEMORANDUM piqued my interest a little more:
*"Regarding Jessica Fletcher's murder mystery seminar.
Let's milk it for all we can, trade off on her name as
much as possible. I suggest we open it up to the public.
Charge top dollar. Bring your ideas on how to market
Fletcher to the afternoon meeting. Michael."*

"Boy, that's pretty sleazy," Jo Jo said.

"See what's on the other disks," I said.

They were blank.

I wasn't sure how to react to what I'd seen and the
fact that the remaining disks didn't contain information. Had the Worrell Institute—more specifically,
Michael O'Neill—deliberately switched disks? Had
Norman's disks been taken by O'Neill?

Or was it a simple mistake? Under the heading of
giving the benefit of the doubt, had the rush of pulling Norm's possessions together for me to pick up resulted in a mix-up?

Dr. Michael O'Neill would have the answers.

"Excuse me," I said, leaving Jo Jo and Jason with
the computer. "Have to make a phone call."

O'Neill said he was delighted to hear from me. He
became almost giddy when I told him I was having
problems with my manuscript, and had decided that
a pleasant dinner out, especially with someone
whose business was helping writers get over their

blocks, made more sense than sitting at my word processor and struggling.

"Tonight?" he said when I suggested I was free.

"Not if it's inconvenient for you," I said.

"Inconvenient? Not at all. And even if it were, Jessica, I would move mountains to make it convenient. Pick you up at seven?"

"That will be fine."

"Le Poisson? I understand it's excellent."

I smiled. "So I've heard. See you at seven."

Jo Jo and Jason were playing a game on Norm's laptop when I returned to the office. "Lunch will be ready soon," I said.

They mumbled an acknowledgment, but their attention was riveted on tiny figures scurrying over the screen.

"I understand from Jo Jo that you're quite a computer whiz, Jason."

Jason looked up. "He said that?"

"I sure did, buddy," Jo Jo said. "I tell everyone that." Jason beamed as he confidently returned to the game.

I'd removed everything from Norm's bag, and had spread it out on my desk. I picked up the label maker and showed it to the boys. I couldn't help but laugh. Norm's obsession with labeling everything in his life included the label maker itself. "LABEL MAKER" it said.

Jo Jo and Jason laughed along with me.

Jason took the labeling machine from me and turned it on. A digital display lit up. "Hey, Mrs. Fletcher, look at this," he said.

Jo Jo and I leaned over Jason's shoulder and read the message on the display.

"WORRELL DOCUMENTARY/SENSITIVE."

"Why would it say something like that?" I asked.

"It was the last label he made," Jason said. "The memory holds on to the last message."

"I see," I said.

"Wonder what it means," Jason said.

"I don't know," I said. "But I have a feeling I'm about to find out."

Le Poisson had been open for less than a year. A New York couple had bought the low, rustic building and converted it into Cabot Cove's most romantic restaurant, at least if your definition of that term has been honed in a Pocono Mountains honeymoon retreat. It's also wildly expensive. New York prices.

The chef, imported from Manhattan, had a nice touch with his dishes, especially seafood. And the main dining room was pretty. Candlelight. Sensuous music from CDs oozed from multiple speakers.

Michael O'Neill and I sat in one of many red velvet booths. Others were occupied by young couples, probably celebrating something special, I decided, their elbows touching, and, often, their lips, as well.

Michael was nicely turned out for our "date." His dark gray three-piece suit looked as if it had been fitted to him just hours before. Not a silver hair on his head was out of place. His complexion was naturally ruddy; this night it looked to have benefited from a facial. It was pink, and soft. I noticed for the first time that his carefully manicured nails were polished. A mark on his negative side.

He'd taken the evening seriously.

I, of course, could not claim to have done the same, and felt a modicum of guilt about it. Not that I hadn't taken time to look presentable. I'd been saving the white silk dress I wore for a special night out. And I had spent more time than usual applying my makeup.

Still, my dishonest reason for being there caused me discomfort. Worse, I couldn't get George Sutherland out of my mind.

George Sutherland.

He was the handsome, urbane Scotland Yard inspector I'd met a few years ago in London during my fateful visit with my friend and reigning queen of mystery writers, Dame Marjorie Ainsworth. A few sparks had flown between George and me, as they say, and we'd kept in touch by mail, and an occasional phone call. He'd planned two trips to the United States, both of which were canceled at the last minute because of cases in which he was involved. I'd planned a trip to London, but a bad case of last-minute flu scotched (no pun intended) that plan. The problem was that George Sutherland was seated next to me in the red velvet booth at Le Poisson, not Michael O'Neill. The psychologists say thinking of someone else while with another isn't unusual—or even bad. I suppose it isn't, but I still wished it weren't the case.

Michael studied the wine list. "Will you be having fish, or red meat?" he asked.

"I—I haven't seen the menu."

"A pink wine would cover all bases, but they lack character and body. Might I suggest a bottle of white? We can go to red later, if your selection calls for it."

"That sounds like a good idea," I said.

"The *Chateau Grillet*," he told the waitress.

We fell into a predictable silence, each of us looking about the dimly lighted room and pretending to be interested in what we saw.

"Well, Jessica, I must admit I was surprised when you called. I had the sinking feeling the past few days that it wasn't your busy schedule that precluded having dinner with me. It was more a matter of not wishing to spend social time together."

"Not true, Michael." To what extent would I be pressed to extend my lie this evening?

"Yes, I know that now. I am delighted to be here with such a beautiful and talented woman. You dress me up, Jessica. But then again, I'm sure I'm not the first man to have told you that."

"Oh, you are. I mean—I'm so glad you chose this restaurant."

"Cabot Cove's best. For Cabot Cove's most illustrious citizen."

"I'm afraid you'll have to stop flattering me. I might begin to believe it." I laughed softly, and wished the wine would arrive.

Which it did, instantly. The waitress, whose golden hair was swept up into a large bun, and who wore a woman's black tuxedo, expertly removed the cork from the bottle, and held it out to Michael. He took it, pursed his lips, inhaled the cork's aroma, and declared the wine to be fit, at least from an olfactory perspective. A small amount was poured into his balloon snifter. Another sniff, a sip, subtle swishing about in his mouth, and a satisfied nod.

"To the beginning of a fulfilling relationship—for both of us."

I clicked my rim to his.

"Shall we order before getting down to serious conversation?" he asked.

"That will be fine."

"Might I order for us both?"

"By all means." I didn't like it when someone else ordered what I was to eat, unless it was in an ethnic restaurant where that other person knew what was outstanding, and what wasn't. But I wasn't about to stand on that principle. The menu, which left prices off the copy handed to me—in this day and age?—was straightforward, steaks and chops, lobster, a few French-sounding dishes, a pasta special, and the usual side orders.

"Caesar salad for two, and chateaubriand for two," he told the waitress. To me: "Rare, Jessica?"

"Medium rare," I said.

"Medium rare it is," he said. "I understand your New York cheesecake is outstanding."

"It's very good," said the waitress.

"Reserve us two pieces for dessert," Michael said.

"I couldn't," I said.

"We'll take it with us," he said. "As a late-night snack. Back at my place."

The waitress raised her eyebrows, smiled at me, and left.

"So, how are things going with you, Jessica? I was sorry to hear that you'd bumped into a wall of sorts in your writing."

"Just a low one," I said. "What's upsetting is that it's never happened to me before."

"Undoubtedly a momentary detour. I would imagine that your friend's unfortunate demise has contributed to it."

"Norman?"

"Yes. Mr. Huffaker was a brilliant man. At least that was the impression I got from our unfortunately short relationship. A grim thought, his body frozen beneath that river."

I shuddered.

He placed his arm over my shoulder, pulled me close.

"How foolish of me, bringing up an unpleasantness on such a pleasant occasion. Forgive me."

A trio of musicians began playing Broadway show tunes, a medley of familiar melodies.

"Aha," Michael proclaimed. "Please." He stood and extended his hand.

I hesitated. I wasn't in the mood for dancing. On the other hand, I'd decided to be there that night with a purpose in mind—to learn what I could about Norman's disappearance, the missing disks, the last entry on his label-making machine, and anything else about the Worrell Institute for Creativity that might help provide me with answers. Feeling very much the Mata Hari of Cabot Cove, I took Michael's hand

and allowed him to lead me to the postage stamp-sized dance floor. The trio was playing "Just in Time" at an easy tempo, and we moved to the pleasant beat.

Please don't dip me, I thought. I hate being dipped.

He didn't, until the band had segued into "Night and Day." As that tune ended, Michael pushed me over and held me hovering above the floor, like an ice-dancing partner.

He laughed as he escorted me to our booth. "Afraid I'd let you fall, Jessica?"

"Never occurred to me for a minute," I said.

We started on our salads.

"A red zinfandel with your beef?" he asked. Without waiting for an answer, he motioned the waitress over and ordered a bottle. "Just coming into vogue," he said to me. "Although, Lord knows why it's taken so long. A worthy wine, less silky than Merlot, which is too soft for my taste, but with sufficient body to please most palates."

"I agree with you completely," I said.

I made a decision in the midst of his monologue on wine.

I was there, at Le Poisson, with him.

I was there for a reason.

Either push it to its limits, or go home.

"Michael," I said, "I haven't been able to find any of Norman Huffaker's computer disks."

He gave me a puzzled look. "I thought I gave them to you," he said.

"I did, too. But the ones included with Norman's laptop were—all blank."

"I don't understand," he said. "I thought—"

"Just a mix-up, I'm sure," I said.

"I'll check into it first thing in the morning."

"I'd appreciate that."

"Or, we could go back to the institute after dinner and take care of it tonight."

"No need for that," I said. "The salad was delicious."

"Nothing better than Caesar. Dance before our entrée arrives?"

"Love to. But no dipping."

"As you say, Jessica."

We spun about the floor with other couples. Michael was a good dancer. I had to give him that. "How is your divorce going?" I asked.

"Dreadfully."

"I'm sorry to hear that. Under the best of circumstances, it can't be pleasant."

"And these are the worst of circumstances. You saw Amanda's behavior on Thanksgiving. I was appalled."

"No need to be."

"A troubled woman, Amanda. I just hope she gets the help she needs."

"I think our dinner has arrived," I said.

Our waitress carved the beef table side.

"You mentioned that my seminar provided some—I think you said 'much-needed cash flow,'" I said.

"Yes. The beef is excellent."

"Very good. Done perfectly. I suppose it's none of my business, but I can't help but be fascinated at how an institute like Worrell supports itself. I suppose there are grants and the like. Government programs—"

"Some."

"Do you get to Washington much, Michael?" I asked, thinking of Norman.

"On occasion. More wine?"

"Worrell is such a large place to run. I can't imagine what the artists pay to be there covers everything."

He laughed heartily. "Hardly," he said, savoring a spear of asparagus.

"I'm surprised you haven't used all the artistic talent you have at hand to raise funds."

"How so? An art exhibition?"

"That would be a wonderful idea. Or a concert. Maybe a documentary that could be shown on television, Public Television, or something."

"An interesting idea, Jessica. I'll bring it up with the staff."

I wasn't sure whether to continue this line of conversation. Why not? I wasn't at the restaurant for a meal. I was there to learn things from Worrell's director.

"Was Norman Huffaker working on some sort of documentary about Worrell?" I asked, tossing the question out as though the answer didn't matter.

O'Neill's face said more than his lack of words ever could. It turned hard. He stared at his plate, then slowly turned to me. "Whatever gave you that idea?" he said.

"Nothing specific," I said. "I just know that he'd recently turned to making television documentaries. I thought he might have—"

"Not about Worrell," Michael said.

I ate as I formulated my next question. I had many to ask. What I wanted to avoid was setting Michael on-edge, cause him to think I'd taken him up on his dinner invitation for mischievous reasons.

"Tell me about this sudden writer's block you've been experiencing, Jessica."

He'd brought the conversation back to solid ground, something with which he'd be more comfortable.

And I saw it as an opportunity. I'd toyed all evening—all day, as a matter of fact, since breakfast with Mort and Seth—with using writer's block as a means of getting closer to the inner workings of Worrell. Would my claim of needing help play with O'Neill, or would he see through it? The only way to find out was to deal that card and see if he picked it up. He'd given me the opening.

"Frankly, Michael, I've never experienced anything like it in my career," I said, injecting what I hoped was an appropriate degree of frustration and concern in my voice. "Oh, I've had an occasional day, maybe even a week, when my writing wasn't going well. When I simply couldn't bring myself to sit in front of my word processor for more than five minutes at a stretch. But this is different. It's been almost a month now that I've been blocked."

"You've certainly hidden it," he said. "I would never have guessed, based upon your unfailingly good spirits."

"I suppose I'm embarrassed about it," I said. "Here I am teaching a seminar on how to write, and the preacher is unable to do what she preaches."

"Do as I say, not as I do."

"Exactly. The thing that's really distressing is that my publisher is upset with me. First time that's ever happened. Vaughan is—his name is Vaughan Buckley. He owns Buckley House—Vaughan is a love, and he's never had to push me to deliver a book. Not that I ever gave him reason to. But this new book is being published to coincide with the anniversary of the discovery of an important archaeological find in Costa Rica. I used that as a basis for the plot."

I touched his hand, and blew a stream of air up into my hair. "Here I am going on about my problems, and you're gentleman enough to indulge me."

"I'm interested in you, Jessica. Professionally. And personally."

"That's very sweet of you, Michael."

"You must eat. Your meal is getting cold."

"I know. I'm sorry."

His hand now took mine, and massaged it. "Let's not have any apologies. I'm just concerned that you're experiencing this problem. Perhaps I could help."

"I don't know how," I said.

"Some time with me at the institute? A long weekend? Focused therapy? It could all be done quietly, and quickly. You aren't like most of the men and women who come to Worrell to get over creative problems. You're a consummate professional. All you need is a few hours, perhaps a few days, of boring in on what is keeping you from completing your book."

"Do you really think so?" I asked.

"I really *know* so."

I couldn't believe how easy it had been. Once I'd decided to try and spend time inside Worrell, I assumed it would take a great deal of pleading and cajoling on my part to get O'Neill to agree.

But here he was opening the door. Maybe I'm a better actress than I've always given myself credit for.

"Are you sure it wouldn't be too much of an imposition?" I asked.

"I would be deeply hurt if you refused," he said.

"I'll pay, of course."

"No, you won't. How wonderful if I were to play some small part in unleashing new and potent creativity in the world's greatest mystery writer."

"You're flattering me again, Michael."

It suddenly occurred to me that I must be coming off as a giggly, dim-witted female. All I needed was a fan to flutter in front of my face as I said, in a Southern accent, "Mah goodness, sir, you flatter me too much, I fear."

I checked his expression. He wasn't viewing me in that light. He seemed pleased with the way things were going.

"This weekend?" he asked.

"Yes. I think that will be fine. I haven't any plans, and—"

"You mentioned, Jessica, at your house on Thanksgiving, that you'd been hypnotized in Boston. That friend of yours, the stage hypnotist."

"That's right. I'm sure you disapprove of him."

"Why?"

"For using such a powerful medical tool for entertainment purposes."

"Not at all. I've seen a number of stage hypnotists. Some of them are as good, maybe even better, than many doctors. What interests me is that you were a good subject."

"Carson seemed pleased," I said. "That's my friend's name. Carson James."

"Aha. I bring this up, Jessica, because I think hypnosis would provide the fastest, and most effective way of breaking through your writing block. Would you be willing to undergo intensive hypnotherapy with me?"

"With you personally?"

"Yes. And some of my staff. Dr. Meti is without peer as a clinical hypnotist."

"I think so."

"Splendid. Now eat your dinner. The beef is prime." He squeezed my hand. "And so are you, my dear."

I anticipated some grappling at the end of the evening. But I was spared that. O'Neill's subtle amorous advances at dinner weren't carried over to bringing me home. He was the perfect gentleman.

"I suggest we keep your date at the institute a secret between you and me," he said as he stood inside my foyer. It had begun to snow heavily, and I expected a suggestion that we share a nightcap in front of the fire. Instead, he said, "I'll call you in the morning, Jessica, and finalize arrangements. Thank you for a lovely evening. It was a pleasure sharing dinner with you."

"The pleasure was all mine."

Chapter Fifteen

The Following Saturday

"Pick you up later, Mrs. Fletcher?" Jake Monroe asked as he delivered me in his taxi to the Worrell Institute for Creativity. It was nine o'clock Saturday morning. The most recent snowstorm hadn't been as severe as forecast. It blew through quickly, leaving a splendid day. Warming sunshine. Brilliant blue sky. White cotton-ball clouds swiftly sliding by overhead.

"No need, Jake. I'm being picked up by—by Dr. Hazlitt."

"Okay," he said. "Help you in with your bags?" I'd brought a small suitcase, and Norman's laptop computer in its padded case. Jo Jo and Jason had shown me how to use it, at least to the extent I could write something on the screen, and store it on the small disk. Of course, I didn't plan to use it. But it seemed sensible to bring the tool of my trade, at least for show.

"No, thank you," I said. I didn't want Jake to know I was staying the weekend. "Just a few manuscripts. Nothing heavy."

As he drove off, I took a deep breath, said under

my breath, "Here goes nothing," and went up the steps.

"Good morning," a slightly overweight young woman with café-au-lait skin at the reception desk said through a wide smile.

"I'm Jessica Fletcher."

"Oh, I don't think you are." Her voice was lightly tinged with her Caribbean heritage.

"Pardon?"

"Dr. O'Neill has you registered under a different name, Mrs. Fletcher. Alexis Peterson."

"Alexis Peterson?" I smiled. "Fine. Then that's who I'll be. At least for this weekend."

"Here you are, Mrs. Peterson. This is your room key. And this booklet explains where things are, and how they work at Worrell."

"Thank you. Is Dr. O'Neill here?"

"He most certainly is. In fact, he's been hovering at the desk for the past twenty minutes hoping to personally greet you. But an important phone call came for him that he took in his office. I'll tell him you've arrived. In the meantime, I'll call Joe to help you with your bags."

"No need to—"

"Jessica!"

Michael O'Neill came down the stairs two at a time. "Forgive me." He kissed me on the cheek, and took my bags.

"You mean Alexis, don't you?"

He put his hand over his mouth, a mock rebuke of his indiscretion. "Oh, of course. I forgot. Yes. Alexis! You don't mind?" He took my elbow and led me to the stairs. "I thought keeping your stay here anonymous was prudent."

"I think it's a good idea," I said as we started to ascend. "I never even thought about it."

"Just trying to be accommodating."

"Which I appreciate. Of course, it would be silly for me to use a false name inside Worrell. I've already met so many people here."

"Yes. But for the outside world—we still get calls from those damnable media people—it would be better to keep your visit private."

"No argument from me. I'd hate for Vaughan Buckley—that's my publisher in New York—to think the advance he's paid me will never result in a book."

We reached the second floor and walked down the empty, silent corridor leading from front to back of the mansion. "It's so quiet," I said. "Everyone in their rooms creating?"

"A few, I suppose. Or sleeping. If I had the time, I'd mount a separate study as to why creative people stay up all night, and sleep all day."

"Not *this* creative person," I said.

"You're the exception, Jessica. Oops. Alexis. Dining room is near empty for breakfast every morning, except for weekends when we have an excellent brunch. Our chef's blueberry pancakes rival Mara's. You'll see."

"I can't wait for morning."

When we reached the end of the hallway, Michael gestured to a door. "Here you go, Jessica. Room Twenty-four. I put you at the end to give you the most privacy." He pulled a ring of keys from his pocket, found the one he sought, and opened the door. I wished he didn't have a key to my room. Nothing unusual for the manager of an inn, or hotel, to have a master key. But considering Michael's professed interest in me, I would have preferred that he not have such easy access to my room. The old chair-propped-under-the-doorknob routine might be in order that night.

Such negative thoughts left me, however, when I stepped inside. The room was flooded with sunshine, washing everything in it—a single bed with a simple white bedspread, four-drawer white dresser, a bleached wooden desk, and a solid, thoroughly uncomfortable-looking wooden desk chair—in pleasant, uplifting light.

The blinds at the oversize window had been rolled up. I looked out on an endless row of tall, stately pine trees rustling in the breeze. "The view is lovely, Michael. So peaceful."

"My favorite room in the mansion," he said. "It's the most private and, believe it or not, one of the largest."

I grinned. It was hard to believe that this room, approximately the size of the walk-in closet in my bedroom at home, was bigger than most at Worrell. "Size doesn't matter," I said. "Somehow, I have the feeling that the simple act of spending two days in this room will work wonders for me and my writing."

Michael sat on the end of the bed. He laughed, not at anything specific, but because he seemed to be in an especially good mood. "Jessica," he said, "I had a marvelous time at dinner the other night. I haven't danced like that in years. Amanda wasn't much for dancing. Of course, as our relationship deteriorated—which happened over a long period of time—dancing was hardly at the top of our activities list."

"I can imagine," I said absently, continuing to gaze out the window. I silently wished he would leave. I wasn't in the mood to be his mother-confessor, his shrink. What happened in his marriage, and its ultimate demise, meant nothing to me.

But I didn't want to offend him by summarily cutting him off. I was there to learn everything I could from him about Norman Huffaker, and what his true purpose might have been in coming to the Worrell Institute.

"I knew at dinner, Jessica, that you and I would find some wonderful common ground," he continued. "That's one of the reasons I'm delighted you decided to spend the weekend with me." (With *me*? I thought). "It will give us a better opportunity to really get to know one another."

"I hadn't—thought of it that way," I said.

"Almost like living together, isn't it?" He laughed. "My mother would never have approved."

I turned to face him. Time to get the conversation back on my alleged writer's block. "This is all so pleasant," I said. "But I musn't forget the serious reason for my being here. I try to ignore this problem I've developed recently with my work, but it's never far from the surface." I bit my bottom lip to indicate trying to hold back a tear, and looked at him with what I hoped would be perceived as desperate eyes. I was acting; my appreciation of what actors do every day increased tenfold.

"It's been hard, hasn't it?" Michael said, his voice sympathetic. He patted the bed next to him. "Come. Sit down."

I shifted into an agitated state, paced the room, wrung my hands. "What I hope," I said, "is that my locking myself in this room for a few days, with no interruptions, I'll break through this creative logjam and begin writing again."

"And I'll be with you every step of the way."

"I know that, Michael. I'm counting on our therapeutic sessions to help, too."

Someone knocked at the door.

"Come in," I said.

A lanky, older gentleman, with long, mouse-colored hair, and wearing glasses tethered to his neck by a red ribbon, stood with a tray on which sat a pitcher of ice water, and two glasses. I motioned him in, and indicated the dresser. As he placed the tray on it, I opened my purse.

"No, Jessica," O'Neill said. "No tipping at Worrell. Thank you, Joe."

Joe closed the door behind him. Unfortunately, O'Neill didn't leave with him.

"Michael," I said, "I've had one heck of a headache since I got up this morning. Would you be offended if I asked you to leave so I can get in a nap?"

He stood. "Of course not, Jessica. I understand. You rest. We'll get together in, say, an hour? Will that give you sufficient time alone?"

"That will be fine," I said. "Thanks for understanding."

"I am, after all, a psychiatrist. Understanding is what I've been trained to be."

I smiled. "Of course," I said. "See you in an hour. Where?"

"I'll come by and pick you up." He closed the blinds on my window, patted my pillow, and backed out of the room.

The moment he was gone, I unpacked my small suitcase and placed the few hang-up clothes I'd brought with me in the tiny closet. I opened the blinds and stood at the window to once again admire the view, which was pure, innocent, and tranquil. I opened the window, inhaled deeply, and focused more intently on the trees, as though they contained the answers I sought about Norman Huffaker—and what was really going on at the Worrell Institute.

Where on earth are you, Norman?

The trees answered with their noncommittal swaying.

I unzipped the padded bag, placed Norm's computer on the desk, and put paper, pens, pencils, and a few paperback books I'd brought along into the single desk drawer. The chair was as uncomfortable as it looked.

I thought of the conversation I'd had with Mort

and Seth the night before. Mort was still enthusiastic about my checking into Worrell. But Seth had a growing list of reservations, the most meaningful that I might be putting my life in danger. "Strange things been happening here," he'd said, his somber face and voice mirroring his concern.

"I'll be fine," I told him. "You two know where I'll be."

"That won't be much help," Seth countered. "After the fact sort of help, if you catch my drift."

At Seth's insistence, we settled on my placing a call to him, or to Mort each day I was at Worrell, at about five in the evening, if possible, without arousing undue notice on Michael O'Neill's part, or his staff. I agreed to it only to placate Seth's concerns. I certainly didn't see the necessity for it.

The only other person I'd told of my plans to spend the weekend at Worrell was Jo Jo Masarowski. But I wasn't honest with him about my reasons for checking in. I told him I needed a few days of uninterrupted concentration, and thought Worrell was just the place to provide it. I wasn't sure he believed me, but he didn't question it. Jo Jo's newfound friend, Jason, knew I'd be away somewhere, and promised to collect my mail and newspapers, and to shovel if another storm hit in my absence. I didn't worry about Jo Jo telling Jason where I was. There's a limit to how many people you can worry about.

I opened the information packet I'd been given at the front desk.

Welcome to **The Worrell Institute for Creativity.**

You've arrived at a very special place, an oasis where the creative acts of writing, singing, composing, sculpting, painting, and dancing, are valued and protected, free from the stress of everyday life.

Worrell is a tranquil, nurturing respite from the outside world. You'll be inspired here by your fellow artists, and benefit from camaraderie with them.

As you create at Worrell, you can enjoy the additional benefit of psychological support from the institute's outstanding professional staff, should a need arise.

We request several things while you are our guests.

First, *that unnecessary noise be kept to a minimum.*

Second, *that you balance your days here between your work, and the peaceful, inspiring surroundings that mark Worrell as a truly extraordinary place. Leisurely walks through the estate's breathtaking grounds, renewal of spirit in our spa, and other amenities ensure that you will derive maximum benefit from your stay.*

Third, *that you slow down, tuck your watch in a dresser drawer, and move through each day accord-*

ing to your inner-clock. *Creativity has never thrived
in a highly-structured, nine-to-five environment.*

I welcome you to **The Worrell Institute for
Creativity.**

*Allow your creative juices to flow. My door is always
open to each of you outstanding bearers of the creative flag.*

> Very truly yours,
> Dr. Michael O'Neill
> Director

"*Bearers of the creative flag?*" What have we come
to, I wondered, as I read the dining room and spa
schedules, which seemed to contradict the advice to
hide your watches and clocks. If you wanted to eat
at Worrell, you'd better know what time it was.

But the spa services were inviting, at least in their
written descriptions. Like a walking example of the
Toyota commercial—"You asked for it, you got
it"—I'd developed the headache I'd lied about to
O'Neill. The Worrell spa offered ammatherapy, a
variation of massage that penetrates pressure points,
allowing energy to flow. I'd once enjoyed that sort of
massage at an Arizona spa. I dialed the number, but
it was busy.

I was five minutes into a fifteen-minute catnap on
the too-soft mattress when someone knocked.
"Jessica. It's Barbara McCoy."

I slowly got up and moved to the door. A DO NOT

DISTURB sign hung on the inside doorknob. Too late for that now. "Hello, Barbara," I said, straightening my skirt.

"Hi, Mrs. Fletcher." She hesitated, then hugged me, which I thought strange considering we didn't know each other very well. "Sorry to disturb you. You look like you were napping."

"That's all right. Just a few winks before getting into the routine. How did you know I was here? In this room?"

"Everybody knows you checked in. Mrs. Peterson, they're calling you."

"Dr. O'Neill's idea," I said. "Well, nice to see you again."

"I just wanted to say hello, and to let you know that I'm down the hall in Room Twenty-one if you need anything."

"That's very kind, Barbara. I haven't been here long enough to know whether I do need anything, or have any questions. But I'm glad to know you're nearby."

"Please don't hesitate. By the way, some of us are having lunch today at the eleven-thirty seating. We have two lunch seatings. Eleven-thirty, and One. Sort of like a cruise ship. We eat in the Thoreau Room." She laughed, and rolled her eyes. "Would you join us?"

"Sounds wonderful. Count me in." I decided that my headache might be due to hunger. An early lunch was appealing.

"See you then," she said happily.

I couldn't help but smile as I had the sudden, and

not unpleasant memory of being back in my college dormitory, girls always knocking at the door to borrow a favorite sweater, or seeking boyfriend advice. But then I remembered the communal bathroom shared by everyone at college.

I quickly scanned the room. To my relief, there was a small door that I'd yet to open. I turned the knob and stared into a dollhouse version of a bathroom. There was a toilet, which didn't seem to conform to regulation size, if there was such a thing in the plumbing world, and a stall shower, more aptly termed a squat shower. The roof over it slanted dramatically to form an isosceles triangle with the floor.

Only for a few days, I thought. Kind of fun.

Then, I remembered that O'Neill had said he'd come back to fetch me in an hour. That posed a conflict with my lunch plans. I was pondering what to do when he appeared.

"You're early," I said.

"And bearing bad news, Jessica. Something's come up. I'll have to postpone our getting together."

"What a shame. I was looking forward to getting started as quickly as possible."

"My sincere apologies. Just a few hours. Would you like lunch in your room?"

"No, thank you. I'm sure I'll manage to meet up with someone I know."

"Of course you will. I keep forgetting how many people you've already met here. Well, until later." He kissed my hand. Actually kissed it. And winked at me. Actually winked at me.

The moment he was gone, I tried the spa number again. "This is Mrs.—Peterson, in Twenty-four. Can you accommodate me for an ammatherapy massage at one? You can? Wonderful."

The Thoreau Room was doing good business when I arrived. To my disappointment, Barbara McCoy was alone at a table. She waved me to it. "I waited for you before getting in line," she said.

"You shouldn't have," I said, looking around the room at tables occupied by three and four people. "Your friends aren't here yet?"

"I don't know where they are." She sounded angry, and I got the impression that she wasn't being joined by anyone—except me. The quintessential unpopular "student"? Every dorm has one.

I followed her to the serving line, spotted a salad bar, and headed for that. Might as well lose a few pounds while there.

Back at the table, I asked how things were going with her music.

"I'm leaving tomorrow," she said.

"Wonderful," I said, sounding as though I was congratulating a mentally ill person about to be released back into society.

"I've had it here," she said.

"Oh?"

"No one will believe me when I say Maureen Beaumont stole my score."

"That's right," I said. "You feel she committed suicide out of guilt for having done that."

"Exactly, Jessica."

"And so you're leaving because of that."

"Yes. And because the staff, especially *him,* feels I'm a disruptive influence with the other artists."

I looked in the direction of her head nod. Dr. Tomar Meti stood at the perimeter of the room, arms folded across his chest, a stern expression on his thin, chiseled face. He looked like a monitor in a grade-school cafeteria.

I didn't doubt that Barbara McCoy was a disruptive influence, and a paranoid one at that. I didn't say that, of course. I ate my salad and allowed her to go on about how misunderstood she was, and how Dr. Meti, along with unnamed others, had made her life miserable since arriving at Worrell. "They decided the minute I arrived that I didn't have talent."

"That's terrible," I said, "considering they're supposed to nurture talent."

"Exactly. I knew you'd understand, Jessica, being the creative and successful person you are."

I speared a cherry tomato.

"It was Maureen who didn't have the talent. That's why she stole my work. God, I—"

"Yes?"

"I'm almost happy she's dead."

"I'm sure you don't mean that, Barbara. Tell me, you've been here during all of it." She looked at me quizzically. "Maureen's death—suicide—the other young woman's attempted suicide, and Norman Huffaker's disappearance."

"You mean *his* suicide, too."

"Yes, I suppose I do. Did you get to know him while he was here?"

"Not well. He stayed by himself. Frankly, I think he came here just to play around. I never saw him do any work. Write, that is. He was supposed to be working on a screenplay. It seemed to me all he did was snoop around and ask questions."

"Ask questions? Of you?"

"Everybody."

"Questions about what?"

She shrugged. "How things work here. Our experiences. He really had a fixation on Maureen."

"But she was dead before he arrived."

"I know. But he kept asking whether we thought she'd really killed herself, or if she might have been murdered."

"What do most people think?" I asked.

"About Maureen? She killed herself. I already told you why."

"That's true. You did. Well, Barbara, I have a date for a massage. Hate to eat and run."

"You and Norman were good buddies, weren't you, Jessica?"

"Yes, we were."

"I bet you took it pretty hard, him jumping in the river like he did."

"Very hard."

She smiled. "What I liked was that he stole Meti's

car to do it." I looked to where Meti had been standing. He was gone.

"I really have to go, Barbara. Best of luck to you in your career."

"Thanks, Jessica. You'll read about me one day. I do have talent, no matter what they say."

"I don't doubt it for a minute."

As I exited the dining room, Dr. Meti was standing in the hallway. "Enjoy your lunch, Mrs. Peterson?" he asked, his solemn mask never changing.

"Very much."

"Ms. McCoy is a disturbed young woman," he said.

"Oh? She said she's leaving."

"That's right. Has Dr. O'Neill gotten back to you about this afternoon?"

"No. I'm on my way to the spa for a massage."

"We'd like to get started with your hypnotic sessions," he said.

"So soon?"

"The sooner the better, Mrs. Peterson."

"All right. I would like my massage, however. I have a headache. It would make it difficult for me to concentrate during the sessions."

"Three o'clock?"

"Three o'clock."

"In the Session Room."

"Which is where?"

He told me and walked away.

The imposing door that read SESSIONS was closed. I knocked.

"Come in."

Michael O'Neill sat in a large, comfortable, over-stuffed, paisley armchair, the kind that envelops you. He looked small in it.

"Hello, Jessica," he said, his fingertips forming a tent over his chest. "Enjoy your massage?"

"It was heavenly."

"Good. Ready for your first session?" His voice, usually tending to rising inflections and exuberance, was low and well-modulated, which I ascribed to the professional setting I'd entered.

"I think so."

"Fine. Fine. Let's proceed."

He took a leather-bound notebook from a small table next to him and began to write. Without looking up, he said, "We'll get started as I do with all patients."

"Patients? I don't consider myself a patient."

He still didn't look up. "Sorry. Too many years as a doctor. Writer. Artist. Let's call this a getting-to-know-you session." Now, our eyes met briefly. He returned to his notebook. "Let's cover the basics, Jessica. Where you come from, something about your parents and siblings, your schooling, hobbies, friends, sicknesses you've had over the years, relationships, marriages, children." He exhibited his first smile since I'd entered the room. "You get the idea," he said.

I nodded.

"So, where is the home of this famous writer of mystery novels? Has it become a tourist attraction?"

"I'm afraid not. I was born in a little town in

northern New Hampshire. Farn, New Hampshire. I understand the house still stands, but not for tourists."

"Your parents?" Michael asked.

I was tempted to say that my personal life was none of his business. But that would have interfered with my purpose in being there.

"My parents are both dead. And no sisters or brothers."

"Your childhood?" he asked.

"What about it?"

"Good? Bad? Happy? Sad?"

"I really don't see why—"

Easy, Jessica, I reminded myself. Focus on your reasons for being here. Cooperate. Nothing gained by alienating him.

"I had a happy childhood, Michael. Traditional. Loving. Caring. Nurturing. Can't blame my writer's block on that."

"This writer's block, Jessica. Tell me more about it."

I was glad we were on to other things.

"Lately, when I sit down to write, I sometimes cry," I said. "I wish my words would flow as fast and gently as my tears." I'd rehearsed what I intended to say about my alleged writer's block. Hopefully, I wouldn't overdo it.

I continued: "I don't know why I cry. A sadness takes over. I always felt that being able to write was a privilege. But lately, it's become a sentence. I sometimes sit in my office—my cell—for hours, without writing a word. Without doing anything.

Like prisoners do in prison. Nothing. Just staring at a blank wall, in my case a blank screen."

"I didn't realize just how severe it was, Jessica. Of course, as you're undoubtedly aware, depression is very much a part of any creative block, both as cause and effect. The level of depression into which blocked creative people sink varies with the individual. In your case, my initial reaction is that your depression is very serious, indeed."

"Really?"

"Yes. The visual image you've created of being a prisoner, in prison, is quite symptomatic."

"I didn't realize it was *that* bad," I said.

Maybe I'd gone too far in describing my contrived dilemma.

"Let's get you started on medication. With today's wonderful antidepressant drugs, there's simply no need to suffer as you have. I'll be right back." He got up and started for the door.

"No, Michael."

He turned to me. His expression was severe.

"I never take medicine," I said. "Not even aspirin."

"An old-fashioned concept, Jessica, and certainly without justification."

I smiled. "I suppose you're right."

What do I do now? I asked myself. He would most likely return with pills I didn't intend to take, and a glass of water to ensure that I did in his presence.

The door opened. "Michael," I said, standing, "I'm feeling nauseous all of a sudden. I wonder if I'm coming down with something. The flu perhaps. You'll have to excuse me. I need to go to my room."

"I'm so sorry, Jessica. Here. Take these pills first." They were in his extended palm. His other hand held the glass of water.

I made the best sick face I could. "Michael, the thought of ingesting anything is too difficult. Please have them delivered to my room."

"Of course, Jessica. I'll send up some medicine for your nausea, too."

"That will be wonderful."

I departed quickly and went directly to my room. A bottle of pills, and Pepto-Bismol, was delivered a few minutes later by Joe, the elderly bellhop. I tipped him ten dollars, which he took without hesitation.

The phone rang.

"Jessica. Michael. Feeling better?"

"Not yet, but the Pepto will help. Thank you."

"The minute you're feeling up to it, be sure to take the antidepressant medicine. Believe me, it will make you feel considerably brighter. In fact, I insist that you take it. It's very difficult to conduct an effective hypnotherapy session with someone as depressed you are. Promise?"

"Promise."

"I've scheduled a marathon session for you tomorrow with doctors Meti, Fechter, and myself. I want you to feel tip-top for it. I've discussed it with them, and we agree that a concerted, extended session is the best approach."

"Whatever you say, Michael. After all, you're the doctor."

"That's the right attitude. Will I see you later?"

"Probably not. If I can manage some soup, I'll bring it to my room from the cafeteria. If not, a solid night's sleep will do the trick. Thank you again, Michael, for all your courtesies."

"Nothing too good for my favorite lady."

I let the line slide.

"In the event I don't see you until tomorrow, be at the Session Room, where we were today, at ten sharp."

"You can count on me," I said.

"Of course I can. Feel better. If you need anything—and I stress *anything*—call the night person at the desk. Since Amanda and I separated, I'm living right here at Worrell. Convenient for me. And for you."

I brought dinner to my room, but not soup or tea. I was hungry, and ordered a full meal, carried it quickly up the stairs and down the hall, hoping I wouldn't bump into O'Neill.

After dinner, I toyed with the idea of taking a walk around the mansion. But I became engrossed in a David Willis McCullough murder mystery I'd brought with me. Next thing I knew, it was a few minutes after midnight. My eyes had begun to close, and bed was intensely inviting.

I was about to change into pajamas when someone knocked on the door. The DO NOT DISTURB sign still dangled from the inside doorknob. "Stupid," I said aloud. Was it O'Neill? I'd pretend I was asleep.

Another knock. "Jess?" A female's voice.

It was the blond fledgling mystery writer, Susan Dalton, who wore black slacks, black sweater, and black sneakers. She looked like a cat burglar.

"Hello, Susan."

"I hope I'm not too late," she said.

"Too late? For what? And yes, you are late."

"I'm sorry. I just couldn't wait to talk to you. I stayed away all day because there's always somebody watching. The staff's asleep by now. Can I come in?" She's said everything in an exaggerated whisper.

"Yes." I stepped back to allow her to enter, which she did, but only after carefully looking up and down the hall.

"Is something wrong?" I asked once we were both inside.

"Lots wrong."

"Oh?"

"I have something to show you. Look!"

She took out a plastic sandwich bag. In it was a key.

"A key," I said.

"You bet."

"A key to what?"

"I'll show you. Put on your shoes. Sneakers if you have them."

"I don't have sneakers."

"Shoes, then. Quiet ones, with soft soles."

"Susan—"

"I know. I'm acting strange, and you're wondering what in the world I'm up to."

"Something like that," I said, failing to stifle a bemused smile.

"Will you come with me?" Susan asked.

"At this hour?"

"It's perfect. Everyone's asleep. At least the staff."

"Where are we going?"

"You'll see."

When I didn't follow her to the door, she said in a slightly exasperated tone, "This key opens up a room in which there is a safe. And in that safe is something amazing, Jessica. Awesome. At least for me, and I know for you, being a fellow writer. Come on." She grabbed my arm.

"You opened this safe, Susan?"

"Yeah."

"How did you know the combination?"

"Inside sources. I'll tell you about that later. Come on."

"Did it ever occur to you, Susan, that opening someone else's safe just might be illegal?"

"It's research. For my novel. Everything's falling into place. What's in the safe gives me a great closing scene. It's so good, I might even become the next you. P-l-e-a-s-e. Let's go now."

"Okay," I said. "Lead on." I slipped into felt-soled slippers and followed her out the door.

Once in the hallway, Susan put her index finger to her lips to remind me to be quiet. We walked slowly and silently, lifting each foot and bringing it down with great deliberation, like old people walking on ice. I heard my own breathing as we proceeded down the corridor. A succession of DO NOT DISTURB signs hung from doors.

Susan led us around a corner, then up a short, narrow flight of stairs that ended at another hall, one I hadn't seen before. Halfway down its length, she halted in front of an unmarked door. Susan withdrew the key from its plastic pouch, inserted it in the lock, and the door swung open. She fumbled in search of a light switch, found it, and the room was illuminated from a low-wattage bulb in a small glass ceiling dome.

The room was in disarray. There were many boxes on the floor, some sealed, some open and empty. A couple of broken chairs and desks lined one wall. It was obviously a room used for storage.

Susan pointed to a far corner. "There it is," she whispered. I followed her. Light from the overhead fixture barely reached the corner, in which a small, old-fashioned safe was nestled.

Susan fell to her knees, pulled a pencil-thin flashlight from a pocket in her slacks, and handed it to me. I directed its intense, focused beam on the combination dial as she quickly, deftly spun it with one hand, using her other to again remind me to be quiet.

The safe opened. Susan peered into its dark recesses, reached inside, and pulled out a file folder thick with papers. She handed it to me. I didn't open it.

"Give it to me," she said. "I'll show you."

She opened the file and nodded affirmatively. "Here. Check this out."

At the top of a piece of gray stationery was the Central Intelligence Agency's insignia. The subject of the letter read: *"Operation Artiste."*

Why would the CIA run a program called Operation Artiste? I silently wondered.

"Go ahead, Mrs. Fletcher. Read."

As I read that letter, and others, all addressed to Michael O'Neill as director of the Worrell Institute for Creativity—and feeling very much the traitor to my country; each document was stamped TOP SECRET—a picture emerged of a remarkable relationship between America's preeminent intelligence organization, and Worrell. It appeared to me—and I admit reading quickly, scanning actually—that Worrell had been established as a center of mind-control experimentation for the CIA. The letters I read didn't specify sums, but it was obvious that Worrell's major funding did not come from its artists-in-residence. It came from the government.

"This is fascinating," I said.

"Read it all," Susan said, sitting on the floor, her back against the wall

I pulled another paper from the file. It's subject was "Maureen Beaumont." It was a memo written by O'Neill to someone at the CIA, in Langley, Virginia.

I'd only gotten a few lines into it when we I heard a noise. "What's that?" I asked.

"I don't know," she said, scrambling to her feet.

"Better put these back," I said. She shoved the

file into the safe, closed the door, and spun the dial.

We left the room. Susan locked the door, and we retraced our steps back to my room. Inside it, and out of breath, she grinned and said, "What do you think of *that*?"

"I don't know what to think of it," I said. "I wish we'd had more time there."

"We can go back tomorrow night."

"I'm not sure I'll be here tomorrow night."

"That's okay. Maybe I can sneak the file out somewhere, have it copied."

"I wouldn't do that," I said. "As fascinating as it is, we have no business, or right, to be reading such documents."

She guffawed. "Jessica, we are witness to what might be the crime of the century. I've read more of the file than you have. We're guinea pigs here. The CIA wants to see if creative people are better subjects to become robots, hypnotized, drugged robots to do the government's bidding."

"Are you sure?"

"Positive."

"Susan, do not remove that file. Forget morality or ethics. It could cost you your life."

"Like it cost Maureen Beaumont her life."

"I think you'd better leave now," I said. "Get to bed. I'll do the same. We can talk again tomorrow."

"Want to meet me somewhere? In town? That place, Mara's?"

"No. I'm meeting most of the day with Dr. O'Neill and his staff."

"I'll hook up with you in some way," she said. She went to my door, placed her hand on the knob, turned, and said, "Be careful, Jessica. These people are evil."

I wasn't sure I'd be able to sleep. But I did. My final thought as I drifted off was that I hadn't called Seth or Mort, as promised. I'd do it first thing in the morning.

Chapter Sixteen

I awoke at six feeling refreshed. I'd only slept five hours, but they'd evidently been hours of sufficient quality to rejuvenate mind and body.

I stopped at the front desk in search of a newspaper on my way to breakfast. The night manager, a slender, pouty young man, was still on duty. "Mrs. Peterson," he said. "You have two messages."

I read the slips he handed me. Seth and Mort had both called, and wanted me to return their calls ASAP.

"That sheriff is a nasty guy," the manager said. "He went ballistic when I told him there was no Mrs. Fletcher here."

"Yes, I imagine he did." It had never occurred to me that they would ask for me by name, but be told no such person existed at Worrell. "Did you finally tell them I was here?" I asked.

"Yeah. After that crazy sheriff threatened to come here and arrest me."

I kept my smile to myself.

"You'd better call them back, Mrs. Peterson. Before the sheriff freaks out again."

I used the pay phone in the lobby.

"Mort? It's Jessica."

"You gave me and Seth some scare," he snapped. "What in hell's goin' on there? Mrs. Peterson. Who's that?"

"That's me, I'm afraid. Look, Mort, I'm sorry about the mix-up, and that I forgot to call last evening. But I'm fine. If things go the way I hope, I'll be back home tonight."

"That's good to hear, Jess. Seth's upset, too."

"Please call him for me. I'm due at a—at a meeting most of the day."

"Learnin' anything?" Mort asked.

"I can't talk, Mort. I'll call later, hopefully from home."

"Unless you forget."

"I won't *forget*. Bye. Have to run."

O'Neill had been right. I was virtually alone for breakfast at that early hour. Brunch wouldn't be served until eleven. Disappointed that I would miss the chef's highly touted blueberry pancakes—I had a waffle, bacon, and juice—I returned to my room, sat at the desk, and, using Norman's laptop computer, made notes about what I'd learned the night before with Susan Dalton, and the conclusions I'd reached at this juncture.

Norman Huffaker was alive. He'd staged his suicide at the Moose River, then driven his Rent-a-Wreck to Boston where he took a flight, under the name B. K. Praether, to Washington, D.C.

He'd come to the Worrell Institute for Creativity under false pretenses. Barbara McCoy had hinted at that during our lunch together. Based upon the left-over label in his label-making machine, he was working on some sort of a documentary about Worrell. My guess was that he'd learned about the institute's connection with the Central Intelligence Agency, and was researching that.

He showed what Barbara McCoy considered an inordinate interest in Maureen Beaumont, the young musician who allegedly took her own life. Ms. Beaumont was from Los Angeles. Maybe they knew each other. Maybe—just maybe she'd come to Worrell under false pretenses, too, to help gather material for Norm. That would mean, of course, that they knew each other well in Los Angeles. I had no information to establish that. Not yet, anyway.

Another suicide attempt, fortunately an unsuccessful one, had left the victim in a semi-comatose state. Coincidence? Possibly. Maybe she had actually tried to take her life in response to Maureen Beaumont's tragic death.

Norm's computer disks had disappeared. Two possibilities. One, they'd been taken by Michael O'Neill and his staff to cover up what Norm had discovered about their CIA connections. Or, two, Norm had taken them with him. I voted for the latter.

According to Susan Dalton, the residents of Worrell were guinea pigs. "Operation Artiste." To see whether creative people made better subjects for mind control. Far-fetched? Perhaps. But I'd read about those horrible experiments conducted by the CIA a few decades ago, in which innocent lives had been lost. Congress had investigated, and demanded that the abuses stop. The CIA had assured Congress all such experimentation was a thing of the past. But was it? Not according to Susan, or the few letters and memos in the file upstairs I'd managed to read.

I stored my notes, and went to the window. Yesterday's sunshine had given way to low, fast-moving gray clouds. It had begun to rain, and the wind had picked up, sending raindrops against my windowpane. At least it wasn't more snow, I thought. The temperature must have risen.

I leaned closer to the window, which afforded me a view to my left of a portion of the circular driveway that wound around the main building, and disappeared in back. A large, black umbrella appeared, presumably from a rear door. It was followed by other black umbrellas. A car—dark green, four-door sedan—came from behind the mansion and stopped where the umbrellas stood. Doors opened, and umbrellas were lowered. Two men in raincoats shook O'Neill's hand, and climbed into the vehicle. O'Neill watched as the car slowly pulled away and passed directly beneath my window. I couldn't clearly make out what was written on the side of the car, but it had a small, official seal of some sort on its door. A government-issue automobile.

O'Neill disappeared from view.

I checked my watch. Ten minutes until my session with him and his colleagues. For a moment, I considered packing up and leaving. Getting out of there.

But I knew I'd be leaving empty-handed, despite what I'd already learned. What could I prove? Nothing. I would go home and wait to learn what had happened to Norman Huffaker. If my suppositions were wrong, that wait would extend until spring, when the river thawed.

A knock at the door.

"Dr. O'Neill asked me to escort you to your session this morning, Mrs. Peterson." Beth Anne Portledge was dressed in her "uniform"—severely tailored dark brown suit, white blouse that buttoned to the neck, and sensible shoes.

"Oh. I was just about to leave for it."

I gathered a few things and fell in behind her down the hall. She knocked at the door marked SESSIONS, heard O'Neill say, "Come in," and held the door open for me.

O'Neill, and doctors Tomar Meti and Donald Fechter, sat in three leather director's chairs that had been arranged in a semicircle. An empty, comfortable leather chair with arms, faced them.

"Good morning, Jessica," O'Neill said pleasantly. "You know my colleagues."

"I've met them."

"Shame the weather has turned," said O'Neill.

"Better rain than snow," I said.

"I see the glass is half-full this morning. That medication I prescribed for you works wonders."

I nodded. The pills I was supposed to have taken were lost in the sewer lines by now. I sat in the empty chair.

"Well, shall we begin?" O'Neill said.

"I suppose so," I said.

"Tomar?"

Meti's eyes were at half mast; he looked as if he

were dozing off. He wasn't. I judged that expression to be his professional, stern "look."

"Mrs. Fletcher," Meti began, his Hungarian accent thick, "it is first necessary to do what we call an Hypnotic Induction Profile on you."

"The one developed by Dr. Spiegel in New York?" I said, remembering the conversation in Boston with Carson James, and Seth Hazlitt.

O'Neill laughed. "How would you know about that, Jessica?"

"I read about it somewhere."

Meti seemed annoyed.

"I didn't mean to interrupt," I said.

"No matter," Meti said. "Let me begin. Are you comfortable?"

"Very."

"Good. I want you to listen very carefully to what I am about to say."

"All right."

"I want you to take a series of deep breaths, allowing the air to come out slowly, very slowly." I did as instructed.

"Now, I want you to roll your eyes up to the ceiling." He placed his fingertips on my hair.

I tried to do what he'd asked, but evidently failed, judging by his angry tone. "Not your head," he said. "Do not raise your head. Just your eyes, while you keep your head level. Roll just your eyes up. As high as you can without moving your head, and hold them up there."

"Very good, Jessica," O'Neill said.

Meti continued: "Now, with your eyes still looking

up, and your head straight and level, s-l-o-w-l-y close your eyelids. Yes. That's right. S-l-o-w-l-y roll your eyelids over your eyes."

"Excellent," Dr. Fechter said.

"Thank you," I said.

"A four, I would say," Meti commented.

"Three to four," Fechter said.

"Mid-range" was O'Neill's verdict.

I opened my eyes. "If you don't mind," I said, "what do you mean by a three or four?" I was thinking of Bo Derek's famous *Ten*.

"Just a test to determine how good a subject you will be for hypnosis," O'Neill explained. "The scale runs from one to five. A 'five' is highly unusual. An extremely hypnotizable person. You fall into the middle range, bordering on its higher level."

"You can tell that just by having me look up?" I asked.

"Yes. There is a physical correlation between the ability to roll one's eyes up high, closing the lids over them while they remain raised, and a subject's hypnotizability."

"Fascinating," I said. I looked at Meti and Fechter, neither of whom seemed pleased at my questions. O'Neill sensed their annoyance, too. "Proceed, Tomar," he said. "Jessica is a highly intelligent, and naturally curious person." To me: "Although intelligence has little bearing on the ability to be hypnotized, brighter people tend to be better able to concentrate, to focus. And that, after all, is what hypnosis is—the ability to concentrate on something, blocking out all other things."

"Interesting," I said. "Will you have me block out my writer's block?"

"Something like that," Fechter said.

"Dr. Meti," I said, "I'm ready for the next step."

My body language must have said something else, because O'Neill leaned forward and took my hand. "You have nothing to be concerned about," he said. "You're with friends. We are here to help get your writing career back on track. That's why you've come to Worrell."

"Exactly," I said. "Sorry if I seem a little tense. This is all very new to me. I'm not used to giving up control."

"Aha, but you won't be," Fechter said. "A gross misconception on the part of the lay public. You don't give up control. You *take* control when hypnotized."

"I didn't realize that," I said. "That's good to hear. And if I am able to take control of my writing, the block will disappear."

"Exactly," they said in unison.

Fechter nonchalantly lowered the lights and the blinds, making the room seem small and safe.

"Mrs. Fletcher, I want you to roll your eyes up again, hold them there, and lower your eyelids," Meti said. He'd pulled his chair to my side, and had placed his fingers lightly on my right arm. I did as I was told. "That's right," he said. "Breathe easily, in and out. With each breath you will feel lighter and more buoyant."

I felt as though I was back on the stage in Boston, with Carson James inducing my hypnotic trance. Go along with it, Jess, I silently told myself. But keep your mind sharp, no matter what they tell you to do. Pretend to be a good subject. But you can fight it. Maintain control.

"Now, you are feeling sleepy. It's a pleasant sensation." Meti's voice was smooth and modulated, his Hungarian accent adding to its soothing effect.

He did what Carson James had done, asked me to imagine that my right arm was attached to helium-filled balloons, and would rise into the air. Which it did. Easy to go along with that suggestion. No harm in raising my arm, which had become delightfully light, a feather floating in the air.

As Meti continued with his soothing instructions, my body relaxed completely. It was an extremely pleasant state in which to be, no cares, no tension, only the drone of his voice repeating things over and over.

Somewhere, somehow, in this blissful state, I reminded myself to conduct a reality check. I saw that O'Neill and Fechter were sitting in their chairs and watching me. I certainly knew where I was, and what I was doing. I'm being hypnotized, I told myself. Or, at least, they *think* I'm being hypnotized.

Meti talked to me about how my difficulty with writing was now a thing of the past. He went into my status as a best-selling author, the faith my publisher and agent had in me, the eager anticipation by millions of readers for my next book. It was all very comforting, especially when he had me "leave" the chair, and sit in front of my word processor at home. My fingers moved fluidly over the keyboard as the words, the scenes poured out. There was no writer's block in this altered state of consciousness. I was the productive writer I'd always been. I no longer had reason to fear the word processor, to feel a prisoner in a cell staring at a blank wall, a blank screen. "It will be helpful, Mrs. Fletcher, for you to be able to experience on your own, in your home, what has happened here today. All the positive feelings and thoughts you now enjoy must be reinforced on a regular basis. Will you do that? Practice what you have learned here today?"

"Practice?" I said. I was aware that the word was slurred as it left my lips. I also knew that I was smiling, at what I knew not.

"Yes, practice," said Meti. "To help you, I am going to give you this computer disk. On it, all the positive reinforcement you need has been recorded. I want you to put this disk in your computer once each day, beginning tonight. I want you to turn on your computer, place the disk in the drive, and follow the instructions on it. Will you do that for me—for you?"

"Yes, I will."

"Good. Now, you are going to slowly leave your pleasant state of weightlessness and be yourself again, right in this room with Dr. O'Neill, Dr. Fechter, and me. But before you do, there is something vitally important for you to understand, and to believe. You are not just one person, Mrs. Fletcher. You are two people."

"I am?" My voice had a dreamy quality to it. I knew that, but couldn't inject steel into it, as much as I would have liked to.

"Yes. You are two people. There is the talented, productive writer, Jessica Fletcher. And there is the destructive Jessica Fletcher that wishes to destroy your career."

"Oh."

"The difficulties you have been experiencing in your writing is the evil work of that other person who resides within you. It is that person who has caused you so much pain, and who threatens your career, your very life."

"I—"

"You must rid yourself of that destructive person."

"I—must—rid—myself—of—that—destructive—person."

"That's right, Mrs. Fletcher. You must get rid of that person *forever*."

"I will."

"Exactly. Now, I am going to guide you back to this room, to your friends. And as I do, I am going to give you a present."

A small, soft leather bag was placed in my left hand. I lifted it. It felt heavy.

"I have given you the means to salvage your career and your life, Mrs. Fletcher. You can use it to ensure that this evil, jealous person living inside you is no longer able to threaten you."

"Is it a gun?" I asked.

"Yes. Your very own gun. But you musn't use it except to defend yourself against the bad Jessica Fletcher."

"How will I know—?"

"I have developed a plan for you that will make it

easy for you to know when *she* is present in your life. I am going to give you this disk for your computer. From it, you will see my words on the screen, the same words I have spoken to you here today. It is important that you play that disk once each day, as a reinforcement of the valuable lessons and skills I have taught you. By doing this, you will have me with you at all times, to help you overcome this other person."

"Thank you," I said.

"My thanks will come when you no longer fear the dark force in your life. I want you to begin counting backward, from one to ten. Do it slowly. As you do, you will begin to shift into a consciousness of the here and now."

"Ten, nine—"

"You will remember nothing of what has happened here today. But you will also recognize that when you see, or hear, the word 'artiste,' you will know the evil Jessica has emerged. And you will do away with her for once and for all. You will put the gun to *her* head and pull the trigger. You will kill her."

". . . eight, seven—yes, I will kill her—six, five, four, three, two, one."

"Hello, Jessica," Michael O'Neill said.

"Hello," I said, stretching my arms and legs in front of me, and giving out with a big, prolonged yawn.

"How are you feeling?" Fechter asked.

"Sleepy. So sleepy."

"And you'll sleep well tonight," said O'Neill. "What do you have there?"

"Oh, this? Dr. Meti gave it to me. A present." I

placed the bag containing the gun in my large purse, which rested at the side of my chair.

"Do you know what time it is?" Meti asked.

"No," I said. I assumed I'd been under hypnosis for only a few minutes. But a large clock above O'Neill said I'd been there for almost two hours.

"How about some lunch?" O'Neill asked, standing.

"Sounds wonderful," I said. "Goodbye, Dr. Meti. Dr. Fechter. Thank you for a lovely experience."

I called Seth Hazlitt after lunch and asked if he was free to pick me up. He arrived twenty minutes later.

"Feeling all right, Jessica?" Seth asked as he escorted me into my house.

"Yes. I feel fine. Just sleepy. A bad sleep last night. Strange place and bed and all. I think I'll take a nap."

"Whatever you say. By the way, did you find out anything about Huffaker while you were there?"

"No. But I found out a lot about myself."

"I see. Well, have yourself twenty winks. Give me a call later this afternoon, or evening?"

"Of course. And this time I promise to remember." We both laughed. He kissed my cheek and left. I went straight to my bedroom and, without bothering to undress, was asleep in minutes.

The house was cold when I awoke. Darkness had set in, although there was still a faint glow on the horizon. The day's rain had turned to ice on the trees and power lines, and made the sidewalks and roads hazardous.

I boosted the heat, went to the kitchen to make

myself a cup of tea, and to go through Saturday's mail that Jason had left on the counter. Nothing interesting, with the exception of a short note from my publisher, Vaughan Buckley, hoping that I was riding out the winter in good fashion, and suggesting that I visit New York in the spring for a conference on my next work.

I carried my tea into my office where I'd dropped my overnight bag, and Norm's laptop computer upon returning from Worrell. I sat in my high-backed, leather swivel chair, took a sip of tea, turned on my word processor, and waited for it to boot up. Soon, I had a blank screen in front of me.

I realized that I was suffering from a certain confusion at that moment. Hard to explain. A fuzziness, wanting to do many things, yet unable to take action to begin any of them.

My purse was on the desk. I opened it, reached in, and pulled out the disk Dr. Meti had given me. I was to use it to reinforce the messages given me while under hypnosis. I sat motionless, immobile, the disk held up in front of my face. Insert it, Jess, I told myself. Take advantage of it.

I absently tried to slide the disk into the drive on my word processor. It wouldn't go in. It didn't fit.

Of course it didn't. My word processor took a special-size disk, unique to it.

I opened the padded case containing Norm's laptop, removed the computer, and turned it on. Tiny flashing lights indicated the batteries were drained. I found the AC power cord, and plugged it into the back of the computer, and into a wall socket. I typed in a few commands until that screen, too, glowed to life. Dr. Meti's disk slipped easily into the slot. I accessed that drive, as Jo Jo had taught me to do, and up came, in living color, Dr. Meti's face.

The sight of him startled me. I didn't expect a face. I didn't know what to expect.

A few hits on the down cursor key brought up text, which began:

> *"Hello, Mrs. Fletcher. Dr. Meti here. By the time you read this, your session with me at Worrell will be over, and I trust it went as well as all of us here at the institute expected it to.*
>
> *"This disk is intended to bolster what you learned during the session with us. It is a reinforcement of all the positive things you will have learned. My suggestion is that you review what's on this disk at least once each day, especially when you feel yourself slipping back into the writer's block that prompted you to seek help from us at Worrell."*

I continued to read as I worked the cursor key to keep the text rolling.

> *"You've taken the first, and crucial step, in solving the problem faced by you, and so many other artistes whose creative output is thwarted from time to time—"*

I stared at the screen for what seemed an eternity before again reaching into my purse and removing the small leather bag given me by Meti. It didn't feel as heavy as when I'd accepted it at Worrell.

It had a drawstring, which I undid. I slipped the small revolver from the pouch and weighed it in my palm. I was not a stranger to weapons. I'd seen enough of them in my career to understand how they work, and the destruction they are capable of delivering. I've never owned a weapon, and would never consider purchasing one.

But instead of being repelled by the weapon, I found the feel of it in my hand to be strangely pleasant. I returned my attention to the computer screen: ". . . And so many other ARTISTES . . ."

I put the gun to my head, to my right temple. My fingers tightened on it, my index finger slowly squeezing the trigger.

It happened first with a "POW." Then, a sizzling sound, and the acrid smell of something burning, something electrical. The screen was dark. All lights in the room were extinguished. The electricity had gone out.

I got up to check the circuit breakers in the kitchen, realized I had the gun in my hand, and fell heavily back into my chair. I felt clammy, light-headed. Disoriented.

A figure moved outside my window. I hurried to it, to see who it was, and to find fresh, cold air to breath. The storm window was down; I couldn't budge it. I banged loudly on the window.

The man outside, whose back was toward me, jumped at the sound I made, and turned. "Mrs. Fletcher!" he shouted. It was Myron, a repairman for

Maine Power & Light, who was kept busy in the winter months.

He shouted in order to be heard through the glass. "Mrs. Fletcher, I didn't know you were home. Jason told me you'd gone out of town. Sorry if I disturbed you."

I said nothing. I was numb. I held both hands up to the window.

Myron's face turned ashen. "Whoa, Mrs. Fletcher. What you got there?" His laugh was nervous. "I know I scared you, but you don't need that with me."

I looked at what he saw. I still held the gun in my right hand. I dropped it to the floor. The sharp report as it went off sent me into spasm. Then, the Chinese vase across the room shattered into a thousand pieces, spraying everything with colorful glass confetti.

"Mrs. Fletcher! You okay?"

I nodded. "Yes," I said weakly, my words never leaving the room. I realized he couldn't hear me, so I motioned for him to come around to the front.

"Mrs. Fletcher," he said as we stood in my foyer, "I am really sorry to have frightened you. One of our new men was out on Friday to read your meter. He reported that your safety wire was severed. I figured he did it, but didn't want to fess up. By accident, I mean. Anyway, I needed to come by tonight and check it out. To do that, I had to cut off your electricity for a couple of minutes. If I knew you were home, I'd have knocked to let you know what I was going to do. Jason told me this morning that you were out of town. I'm really sorry. I saw how scared you were and—"

"It's all right, Myron," I said. "Actually, you did a very good thing. You—you saved my life."

"I did?"

"Yes. At least I *think* you did. Why don't you go ahead and fix that broken wire. When you're done, I'll have a hot cup of tea, and some cookies, waiting for you. In the meantime, I have a very important phone call to make."

"To your publisher?" he asked. He'd always been fascinated that I was a writer.

"No. To the sheriff. I think we have some newcomers in Cabot Cove who have a great deal to answer for."

Chapter Seventeen

My call to Sheriff Morton Metzger brought him, two of his deputies, and Seth Hazlitt to my house. When they arrived, Myron, the Maine Power & Light repairman who'd kept me from doing something silly like shooting myself, was enjoying tea and cookies in the kitchen. I'd tried to sweep up what I could of the Chinese vase, but many tiny pieces remained in the carpeting and furniture.

Mort gave Myron a look that said, Time for you to leave, son.

"Great cookies, Mrs. Fletcher," Myron said as he put on his coat. "Good as down at Sassi's. Much obliged."

Mort's deputies examined my office, while I sat with my two friends in the kitchen.

"Let's go over this again, Jessica," Seth said.

"I'll handle the questions, Doc," Mort said.

Seth mumbled something and sat back as I recounted everything that had happened up until the time the gun went off.

"And you say O'Neill and his cronies set you up to shoot yourself through hypnosis?"

"Yes."

"Mind if I interject a question?" Seth asked.

"If you have to," said Mort.

"What I don't understand, Jessica, is that if they were successful in getting you to actually put the gun to your head, how come havin' the electric go off wiped away that posthypnotic suggestion?"

"If I knew the answer to that, Seth, I'd be glad to share it with you. I'd probably write an article on my findings for the *New England Journal of Medicine*. Maybe it was the shock of the screen going blank. Maybe it was the room suddenly becoming dark. All I know is that I held that weapon to my head, and was about to pull the trigger."

"And it was because that word 'artiste' appeared on the screen," Mort said.

"Exactly. I'd be happy to show it to you, except that the power failure blew something in Norman's computer. You'll see it later. But I remember distinctly that Dr. Meti told me that if that word was spoken, or appeared in print, I would want to kill the evil person inside, the 'Jessica Fletcher' who was keeping me from writing."

"Damn shame," Seth said.

"What is?" Mort asked.

"That none of this can be proven. According to Jess, everything she read on the screen was positive reinforcement. Common thing medical hypnotists use. All you've got is her word that the suggestion was planted about the word 'artiste.' "

"We'll see," Mort said, without conviction.

The phone rang. "I don't believe this," I said loudly

into the receiver. "Norman is there? Your *husband*, Norman?"

"Yes," Jill Huffaker said. "Isn't that wonderful?"

"It's better than that," I said. "Where has he been?"

She hesitated before answering, "Washington, D.C. Just like you said, Jess."

"Can I speak with him?"

He came on the line. "Hello, Jess. Had everybody worried for a while, huh?"

"A monumental understatement. What—?"

"All questions answered in person," he said. "Jill and I are catching the red-eye tonight to Boston. Be in Cabot Cove in the morning."

"Why? I mean—"

"No comment—until tomorrow. See you then, Jess."

Mort and Seth stared at me as I hung up. "That was your friend, Huffaker?" Seth said.

"Yes. He's alive. *He's alive!*"

"No explanation?" said Mort.

"Tomorrow. He and Jill are flying in tonight."

I got up to check on how Mort's deputies were doing when a dreadful thought hit me. "Oh, my God," I said.

"What's the matter, Jessica?" Seth and Mort asked.

"Susan Dalton. She's still at Worrell. I'll bet anything that O'Neill and the others knew we'd been up in that storeroom looking at things in the safe. They'll try to kill her, too."

"Not if I have anything to say about it," Mort announced. He instructed his deputies to go to the

Worrell Mansion and remove Ms. Dalton, by force if necessary, from the premises.

"Bring her here," I said. "She can stay with me."

"I'm the mayor of Cabot Cove, and I shall make the opening comments."

Sybil Stewart and Mort Metzger argued in a corner of the town council's main meeting room. I could hear their conversation from where I sat with Seth Hazlitt and Jill Huffaker.

"Seems to me this is a criminal matter," Mort said. "Seems to me the sheriff should run things."

"Well, Sheriff Metzger, what seems to you doesn't 'seem' to me. I'll conduct the conference, and introduce you at the appropriate time. Understood?"

"Yes, ma'am." He looked at me and winced. I turned away; I didn't want to laugh.

Sybil took the podium and asked for silence. When it wasn't forthcoming, her exasperation flared. "If you don't want to hear what we have to say this morning, then I'll call this off, and you all can go home and wonder what you'd missed." A smug smile crossed her thin, tight face.

Seated behind Sybil were Mort, Jared Worrell, who'd flown in overnight, Norman Huffaker, who'd been in town but who'd kept a low profile until this morning, and a man I didn't recognize. He was big and beefy, dressed in an overtly expensive suit, and with high color in his cheeks. His smile was pleasant and open.

"That's better," Sybil said when audience chatter lessened to an acceptable level. "As you all know, a

shocking revelation has been made about the so-
called Worrell Institute for Creativity. Shocking to
most, but not to me. Those who know me are aware
that I took a stand against the Worrell Mansion being used for such purposes from the moment it was
announced."

A few of her more overt supporters clapped.

"Thank you. As it turned out—and despite the efforts of certain people in this community to thwart
an investigation into what was *really* going on at the
mansion, the truth has finally emerged." She paused
for more applause. An elderly man obliged.

Sybil went on to credit her administration with
uncovering the mischief at Worrell, ending her written speech with, "Unfortunately, the life of a talented and promising young woman was snuffed out
in the prime of her life because of the irresponsible,
criminal actions of those who held themselves out as
men of science and medicine. Their misdeeds might
have claimed more lives, were it not for the insistence of my office that our law enforcement officials
keep the case open. Which they did, and for which
we can all sleep easier."

I looked at Mort, whose expression spoke eloquently of his inner discomfort.

"Let me now introduce our sheriff, Chief Metzger,
who will add his own, very brief, comments to what
I have already said."

After clearing his throat a few times, Mort said
into the microphone, "Based upon what we've gathered so far, the Worrell Institute for Creativity wasn't
what it pretended to be. Seems it was established

here in Cabot Cove to carry out some experiments by the Central Intelligence Agency. Seems the folks at the CIA had a theory that people who do creative things, like write and paint and write music, might make better hypnotic subjects, who could be used by our intelligence agencies to do their courier and spy work. The way they figured it, those artistes who were the best subjects wouldn't even know what they were doin'. Worse, one of them, Ms. Maureen Beaumont, was taught to kill herself. Which she did. You all know about that."

"Then it *was* a suicide," a reporter shouted.

"Yup," Mort said. "But not one that involved free will. Everything points to Ms. Beaumont having been programmed to shoot herself. Just like—" He looked at me. I shook my head.

He went on to another topic, to my relief. "I know all of you, especially the media folks in the audience, want to know whether indictments have been brought against the doctors at Worrell. Well, they haven't been. But that doesn't mean they won't be. The three main doctors up on the hill, Michael O'Neill, Tomar Meti, and Donald Fechter, have all left, all gone down to Washington, D.C. Because the federal government is involved, we got ourselves a classic jurisdictional dispute goin' on. But I've been meeting with officials from the state, and the Feds, and we'll get this sorted out lickety-split. I assure you of that. That's about all I have to say this morning. But I'll keep everybody posted."

He turned the podium over to Sybil. She introduced Jared Worrell, who'd sold the mansion to the

Boston developers, the Corcoran Group. They, in turn, had leased it to Michael O'Neill and his people.

"I am well aware of the pain I've caused this wonderful community," Worrell said. "When I made the decision on behalf of my family to sell the mansion to the Corcoran Group, it was because I had absolute faith that it would be put to good and worthwhile use. The people from Corcoran are highly regarded. I know you'll enjoy hearing from a representative who is here today, Matt O'Brien." He pointed to the heavyset man in the nice suit. "All I can say is that the Corcoran Group was as convinced as I was that Dr. O'Neill and his people, whose credentials are—were—pristine, intended for my family's home to be put to a use that would benefit mankind, as well as this community.

"Discussions are now underway for a better future use of the property. For now, thank you for understanding that the motives of all concerned, with the exception of those who created the institute, were good and proper. Thank you."

Matt O'Brien, a gregarious and confident public speaker, basically echoed what Worrell had said. He assured everyone in the room that the next tenant of the Worrell Mansion would be a credit to Cabot Cove. His comments were enthusiastically received.

"And now," Sybil Stewart said, "it is with great pleasure and pride that I introduce a former neighbor, who went on to achieve fame and fortune in Hollywood, and who joins us here today. I might add that the reports of his demise were greatly exagger-

ated." She expected more laughter than she got.
"Please welcome Cabot Cove's own, Norman
Huffaker."

Norman stood at the podium, looked down over
the crowd, and basked in its welcome. When the applause died down, he said, a boyish grin on his face,
"I have a lot to explain to you, especially to my dear
friend, Jessica Fletcher. It's a long story. A *very* long
story. I'll try to give you the *Cliff Notes* version.

He spoke for ten minutes, explaining that he'd become interested in the CIA's resumption of mind-
control experimentation, and had obtained financing
to produce a documentary on it. A source identified
plans for converting the Worrell Mansion into a CIA
think tank, which excited him. Norm knew Cabot
Cove. It seemed a perfect centerpiece for his documentary.

He'd worked on a film in Los Angeles with a
young musician, Maureen Beaumont. When he con-
fided in her about his plans, she volunteered to
check into Worrell to learn what she could about its
inner operations. When she died—and Norm never
bought for a minute that she'd killed herself of her
own free will—he did what he had to do. He
checked in himself.

Everything else he had to say was no surprise to
me. It was what I'd decided had happened—the running car at the river, the note, the rental car waiting,
his clandestine trip to Washington where, he told us,
he'd nailed down what he needed to finish the documentary from an anonymous source within the intelligence community.

Sybil concluded the press conference by taking a string of questions from members of the press. No one on the panel had much to offer in the way of concrete evidence, including Mort.

"Let's leave," I whispered to Seth, "before they start asking *me* questions." "See you back at the house," I whispered in Jill Huffaker's ear.

"It's brilliant, Norman," I said after he'd shown us an unedited version of his video documentary. We sat in my den—Mort Metzger, Seth Hazlitt, Norm and Jill Huffaker, Jared Worrell, Matt O'Brien, Susan Dalton, and Jo Jo Masarowski—whom I'd invited for the private screening. At first, Norman didn't respond. He stared at the TV screen, his eyes misty. He'd used the remote control to freeze a frame of the final credits.

> *Special love and thanks to Maureen Beaumont,*
> *a talented and courageous lady who*
> *gave her life for this documentary.*
>
> *She is very much missed.*

A picture of Maureen accompanied the text. A piece of classical music featuring a flute had provided the documentary's music track.

"Did Maureen compose that music, Norman?" I asked.

Tears welled up in his eyes, and his lip trembled. He nodded. We hugged. I, too, fought back tears.

Later, after everyone had left except the Huffakers, Norm said, "Jessica, I'm very sorry to have put you through what you went through. Sheriff Metzger told me about your weekend at Worrell, the hypnosis, and you coming close to killing yourself."

"It was an adventure." I laughed. "I can sound blasé in retrospect. At the time, I wasn't quite so cavalier."

"I would imagine," Jill said. She looked to Norman, then at me. "I'm afraid I have a very difficult admission to make to you, Jess."

"Really?"

"Yes. All I can hope for is that you'll understand the difficult position we were in when I did it."

"I'll certainly try," I said. "It can't be that bad." They said nothing. "Can it?"

They held hands. Jill said, "I knew Norman wasn't dead."

"So did I," I said.

"You didn't *believe* he was dead. I knew for certain."

"You did? For how long?"

"The entire time," Jill said.

"And you never—"

"Not only that," Norm said, "Jill was the one who planned my escape, how I'd do it, where I would go."

"I think I understand," I said. My sadness at having been strung along by Jill was evident, I knew, in my voice and face.

Jill continued: "When Norman realized they'd gotten on to him, the way they did with Maureen, and knew why he was there, he called me. Together, we decided he would fake his suicide, and get out of there as fast as possible."

"And so you took Meti's BMW to the bridge, left the note, walked to the Rent-a-Wreck, picked up the red Chevy, drove to Logan, and boarded a plane to Washington," I said.

"Right. I met with my source, my 'Deep Throat,' then headed straight for the airport and flew home."

"Every time we spoke on the phone, Jill, you knew that Norm was alive."

"Afraid so, Jess," she said.

"Nine out of ten times I was sitting right next to her," Norm added.

I was torn between expressing anger that a friend would do that to me, and understanding their need to keep Norm's whereabouts a secret, to sustain the suicide story until it was safe to surface.

"Well," I said, "I'd be lying if I didn't admit to being angry with both of you. On the other hand, I'm glad you're alive, Norm, that you got to complete your documentary, and that we can be together again."

"Forgive us then, Jess?" Jill asked. "Forgive *me*?"

"Forgiving is for God, Jill. I'm just a writer. More coffee?"

Chapter Eighteen

"Yes, Mort, I understand," I said.

"Seems the gun Meti gave you was owned privately by him. That might blow holes in his claim that the CIA provided it to him, and that he was doin' official work for the United States government."

"The government seems to be denying any involvement with the Worrell people."

He chuckled. "No surprise there, Jess. You go to work for a spook agency, if you get caught, nobody knows you. You're on your own."

"How cold," I said.

"Just the way it is. By the way, everybody's out of the mansion. The Worrell Institute for Creativity is a thing of the past."

"Glad to hear it. Susan Dalton, and Jo Jo Masarowski, called me. They're back home. Susan is working on her murder mystery, using what happened at Worrell as her plot. Jo Jo says he's developing a video game about hypnosis."

"I can give him a name of a fella at Parker Brothers."

"I'm sure he'd appreciate that."

"Talked to Seth this mornin'. That gal who swallowed all those pills is doin' fine. Seth expects she'll go home in a week or so."

"Then she did try to kill herself, without any suggestion from O'Neill and company."

"Yup. Got so upset over Maureen Beaumont's death that she flipped."

"Well, I'm glad she's doing well. And thanks for the update."

I hung up and went to tend plants in my living room. As I carefully poured water from a long-nozzled watering can, a car pulled up in front of the house. I watched as two men got out, said something to each other, then approached my front door. I opened it before they had a chance to knock.

"Jessica Fletcher?" one of them asked. He was short and slight. He wore a gray tweed jacket, muted green paisley tie, blue button-down shirt, and had a red scarf wrapped around his neck. His glasses were large and round. His hair was blond, and thinning. It raised up in wisps in the wind that whipped about my front patio.

His colleague looked like a policeman out of Central Casting. Big. Square. Short hair. Cheap, green raincoat. Thick-soled black shoes.

"Yes."

The thinner man produced an ID: Special Investigator—Congressional Subcommittee on National Security.

"What can I do for you?" I asked.

"We'd like to speak with you, Mrs. Fletcher. Won't take long."

"About the Worrell Institute?"

"May we come in, ma'am?"

"Of course. I'm sorry."

We settled in the living room. They declined my offer of coffee, or tea.

"You're a famous writer," the thin fellow said.

"I'm a writer. Famous? Maybe."

"You're obviously someone who cares about her country and its future."

"Of course."

"This experience you had at Worrell, Mrs. Fletcher. I understand it was somewhat traumatic."

"It was—it was unsettling. But it's over. The people there—Dr. O'Neill and his staff—caused the death of a young woman, in the name of scientific experimentation."

"An unfortunate incident, Mrs. Fletcher."

I'd begun to resent their presence, and the tone of the conversation. "Unfortunate incident?" That's all it was?

"Dr. O'Neill and his colleagues acted on their own, Mrs. Fletcher."

"That's not the way I see it," I said.

They looked at me as though I'd said something naughty.

"The Worrell Institute for Creativity was funded by a government agency," I said. "The CIA, to be exact."

"Mrs. Fletcher, the congressional committee I work for is charged with overseeing the intelligence activities of the United States. Naturally, we are concerned with any abuse of those activities, especially if they involve average citizens."

"I'm glad to hear that," I said. "Because in the case of the Worrell Institute, average citizens certainly were *involved*."

He had a way of ignoring anything I said. It was annoying, at best.

"Dr. O'Neill and the others involved have claimed a connection with the United States government as a defense for their actions."

"And?"

"We're here to assure you, Mrs. Fletcher, that there was no such connection."

"I don't believe you," I said. "I know different."

Shrugs from both of them.

"O'Neill will be prosecuted for the death of Maureen Beaumont."

"Thrown to the wolves."

Shrugs.

"I would appreciate it, gentlemen, if you would leave now."

They stood. The thin one said—the other had said nothing, and was unlikely to—"The government of the United States sincerely appreciates your discretion in this matter, Mrs. Fletcher. The President of the United States has asked me to personally present this to you." He handed me a large envelope.

"What is it?" I asked.

"A token of appreciation for your patriotism."

"That's very thoughtful," I said, standing and indicating the direction in which the door was located. I accompanied them out to the patio. The larger man looked up into the blue sky, smiled, and uttered his first words: "Looks like spring is here."

"And just in time," I said. "Thank you for stopping by. And please thank the President for his kind gift."

I watched them get into their automobile and drive away, resumed watering my plants, and went to my office where I opened the envelope bearing the Presidential seal. In it was an eight-by-ten color photograph of the President and First Lady, posing on the White House lawn with their Dalmatian, Boopsie, who'd garnered headlines when he bit his master, prompting press cynics to praise the inherent wisdom of dogs. The photo was inscribed to me: *"For Jessica Fletcher. A fellow patriot. God Bless!"*.

I placed the photo into a lower desk drawer, booted up my word processor, waited for the blank screen to appear, and brought up the file: *Brandy & Bullets*. By Jessica Fletcher.

It was good to be working again.

Cross the
Golden Gate Bridge
with America's
favorite sleuth
in the next
Murder, She Wrote
mystery novel:

Martinis & Mayhem
by Jessica Fletcher
& Donald Bain

Coming from Signet
in December 1995

Once George disappeared through the crowd, and buoyed by the thought of having him around for a whole week, I left the Top of the Mark and headed out for some evening sightseeing.

Fisherman's Wharf: I snacked on a crab cocktail from a sidewalk vendor, purchased a lovely tooled-leather address book from a local artisan, and enjoyed a cup of Irish coffee at a communal table in the Buena Vista Cafe, where that scrumptious concoction was first introduced to this country by famed San Francisco columnist, Herb Caen. From there, I hailed a taxi and asked the driver to take me down Lombard Street, "the world's crookedest street," which he did, and which I found to be fun even though I'd done it numerous times before.

My internal dinner bell went off, and I headed for Chinatown, *the* Chinatown, for an appetizer of minced squab wrapped in lettuce leaves, and lobster broiled in ginger sauce, at Celadon.

I arrived back at my hotel, the St. Francis, at eleven feeling wonderful and thought of Abraham Maslow, the pioneering psychologist, who identified one of the signs of sanity as having the ability to recognize and enjoy "peak experiences"—those moments, large or small, when you are at one with the world, and when your senses explode in celebration. A lovely climbing rose bush wet with dew. A sudden snap of cool air after a period of hot and humid weather. A baby's smile. A lick from a loving dog's warm, wet tongue.

The physical beauty of San Francisco. Excellent food. Bracing air. Friendly people. The anticipation of a week with Chief Inspector George Sutherland.

At that moment, according to Maslow, my sanity was beyond debate.

"Good morning, Mrs. Fletcher. It's seven o'clock, and sixty-one sunny degrees outside. Have a wonderful day."

"I certainly intend to," I said to the recorded wake-up message.

I'd decided to skip the gym that morning, and to ease into the day at a more leisurely pace. I'd done plenty of walking the night before. Besides, having decided to take a walk across the Golden Gate Bridge would make up for any lost time on the exercise bike.

It had never occurred to me before to take such a walk. I didn't even know it was possible for pedestrians to cross that famous span.

But Robert Frederickson had suggested it. And the cab driver who'd driven me down the hairpin turns of Lombard Street last night had casually mentioned that crossing the Golden Gate on foot was one of his favorite things to do on a day off.

And so I decided it offered a chance to do something different in a city rife with different things to do.

I wanted an early start; new adventures are always more enjoyable, at least to this early riser, when experienced in the cool, crisp morning air. The vision of the bridge showered in the early morning light was palpably pleasant.

I turned on a small television set in the bathroom, adjusted the water in the shower, got in, shampooed with a lovely almond shampoo provided by the hotel, and was in the act of vigorously washing my hair when I heard the phone ring. Although there was a phone in the bathroom, it was on the opposite wall. I hate decisions like that. Do I step out of the shower and drip water all over the floor? Try to towel off in time to catch who was calling? Ignore it, and let voice mail take a message?

I opted for the latter course of action. It rang seven times. Usually, voice mail picked up in four rings. Maybe it wasn't working, in which case I wouldn't have a message. How frustrating. A waterproof telephone in the shower would have been a welcome amenity.

I dried off with one of the oversized, plush velvet towels that I'd wished weren't bad form to pack in my suitcase, peeked into my bedroom and saw the flashing message light on that room's phone. Wrapped in my luxurious towel, I punched in the numbers to activate voice mail.

"Good morning to you, lovely lady. George here. You've evidently gotten off to an early running start to the day, one of many admirable traits I've observed in you. Unless, of course, you're still sleeping, in which case I take back my compliment and will ring off in order not to disturb your much-needed slumber." He paused to see whether I'd pick up. When I didn't, he continued, "Jessica, the reason I'm calling is to give you the name of the gentleman I'd mentioned last night over drinks. You know, the illustrator for Kimberly Steffer's books. His name is Brett Pearl." He spelled it for me. "I looked the chap up in the phone book and he's listed as living in Sausalito, with an office in downtown San Francisco. Evidently doing quite well, wouldn't you say? Have a good day, as you Americans are fond of saying, and be in touch. 'Bye for now."

I slipped into a terrycloth robe bearing the St. Francis's insignia, went to the desk in the living room and found the white pages. I looked under Pearl. *Pearl, Brett, 508 Birch, Saus.*

Was it fate? I planned to cross the bridge from San Francisco to the Sausalito side. I wasn't sure whether I'd do a roundtrip walk, or take the ferry back to the city. A few hours in the quaint village of Sausalito would give me time to recover and to make that decision. And, of course, to drop in unannounced on Mr. Brett Pearl: "Hi, I was in the neighborhood and thought . . ."

But by the time I was dressed and ready to venture out, I thought better of that plan. Walk across the bridge, Jess, but don't walk into trouble. What was that Scottish expression George Sutherland was fond of using? *"Better make your feet your friends."* Translation: "Run for your life."

The taxi drove away, leaving me standing in awe at the San Francisco side of the almost two-mile-long, breathtaking orange suspension bridge known world-wide as the Golden Gate. If it hadn't been modern, it would certainly qualify as the eighth wonder of the world. It was created by a gentleman named Joseph Strauss, who oversaw the four-and-one-half-year construction project that culminated in 1937 with the punch of a telegraph key 3000 miles away in Washington, D.C. by President Roosevelt. That resulted in horns and whistles, and the biggest peacetime concentration of naval war vessels in history.

I'd read that the bridge was 260 feet high at midpoint in order to allow the Navy's largest battleships to pass beneath it. I'd also read in my handy guidebook that on opening day, and before vehicles were allowed on it, more than 200,000 pedestrians had swamped the bridge, their weight causing the center to drop as much as ten feet. Not to worry; it was designed to survive winds in excess of one hundred miles an hour, and to sway as much as twenty-seven feet at its center.

It wasn't perfect bridge-walking weather. What had started as a sunny, calm day had quickly deteriorated into an overcast, windy one, at least where I stood. I'd dressed for it. You learn to anticipate weather turns in Maine. I wore an ivory cableknit sweater, sweatpants, sneakers, and my red, white, and blue windbreaker.

But I wasn't the only person to be undaunted by the wind and gray skies. Dozens of men, women, and children were on the bridge—some just completing their journeys, others starting out in the direction of Sausalito. I silently hoped they were all there to *walk* the bridge, and not to jump. In some quarters, the Golden Gate Bridge is as famous for those who don't make the return trip, as it is for its beauty.

I looked across the length of the span. Silly, I thought, to feel so much trepidation. Hundreds of people did it everyday. I'm not exactly fond of heights, but I don't have any special aversion to them.

I started out, and soon decided that the biggest threat to my safety were the automobiles whizzing by. The pedestrian walkway wasn't very wide and the cars seemed to be too close for comfort.

I continued. The farther I went, the more spectacular the view became. Although it remained misty on the bridge, shafts of sun seemed to explode from the gray clouds above, spotlighting the city's white and pastel buildings and newer curtainwall skyscrapers. Another shaft played on the millions of ripples in San Francisco Bay. It was spectacular; my gasp was involuntary.

I forged ahead, the wind stinging my face, the slight sway of the bridge beneath my feet actually pleasant, like being on a mighty ocean liner. The bay was dotted with sailboats and a few brave windsurfers, who appeared to be getting knocked about pretty good.

Others on the bridge were in a good mood. Almost everyone smiled as they passed and said something in greeting, which I returned. I felt marvelous. My blood raced as I picked up my pace. How far had I come? I'd estimated it would take about an hour to complete the journey to Vista Point on the Marin County side. I'd been walking for a half hour. That should put me at mid-span. Judging from the cluster of people there, that was exactly the point I'd reached. Dozens of cameras were pointed in every direction.

Despite the number of fellow tourists, I felt pleasantly alone. I could feel my heart beating in my chest, and I wiped at tears caused by the wind. As I drew deep breaths, I felt giddy. Did I look foolish? Childish? No matter. Times in our lives when we get to feel like children again are too precious to let pass.

I slowly turned to take in the panorama of my surroundings. To my left were the hills of Sausalito and Marin County. With my back to the bridge railing, I could see over the traffic the vast expanse of the Pacific Ocean. Another ninety-degree turn and I looked back to the direction from which I'd come. And then I returned to my original position, peering out over San Francisco Bay and across to Berkeley. It was like an Impressionist painting. Pissarro? Monet? Degas? Perhaps Renoir.

What happened next was hardly impressionistic. It was more out of the school of brutal realism.

It started when an especially strong gust of wind caused me to throw back my head and to laugh. I closed my eyes for a second. And then I felt the strength of a hand, connected to a strong arm, grasp the back of my neck and shove me forward. Simultaneously, another hand—presumably belonging to the same person—grabbed the bottom of my windbreaker and attempted to pick me up and push me over the railing.

I fought to maintain a hold. I shouted, but my voice was carried away by the wind, inaudible to even me. I tried to twist in order to see who was trying to push me to my death, but failed.

And then, as suddenly and unexpectedly as this unknown person had come up behind me, he, or she, was gone. I was draped over the railing when the pressure ceased, gasping for breath, shaking uncontrollably. Finally—it seemed minutes, although it was only seconds—I stood and turned, my knees trembling to the extent I wasn't certain they would support me. It had happened so fast that no one, it seemed, had seen the attack. They were too busy marveling at the views, and taking pictures of them.

Except for a young girl, perhaps ten, who said, "Are you okay, lady?"

"Yes. No. I mean—" I looked past her in search of the person who'd tried to kill me. Whoever it was had disappeared into the crowds walking the bridge that morning.

"Did you see who tried to push me over?" I asked her.

"Push you? No, ma'am. You look like you're sick, that's all."

"Sick? No. I'm fine. Thank you for asking."

I knew that if I didn't start walking again, the sudden nausea I was experiencing would worsen. I ruled out continuing to the Sausalito side of the bridge. I wanted to be back in San Francisco, in my suite, safe and secure. I also wanted to report the incident to the police.

Oddly, even though I was in a hurry, I started off walking slower than before in what might have appeared to be slow-motion determination, a drunk making sure each step connected with the ground.

But my need to get off the bridge took over, and I actually began to jog. Me, who has never jogged in her life. And finally, I broke out into a run, as if my life depended on it—which I was fairly certain it did.

I reached the other side in what might have been the fastest mile ever recorded by a female mystery writer from Maine, who was on the wrong side of fifty.